SOMETHING IN THE DARK

A JED HORN STORY

Peter Nealen

This is a work of fiction. Characters, locations, and incidents are products of the author's imagination.

Copyright 2024 Peter Nealen

All rights reserved. No part of this book may be reproduced in any form, or by any electronic or mechanical means, including information storage and retrieval systems, to include, but not exclusive to, audio or visual recordings of any description without permission from the author.

Printed in the United States of America

www.americanpraetorians.com

NOCTURNAL INTRUDER

The eyes can play tricks as much as the mind can, in the dark. Without the amount of light that they're used to, they start to try to fill in details, details that aren't always there. But those illusions are easily dismissed as such once you get another look, even when sleep deprived.

When I looked straight at the smoky light moving along the riverbank, it didn't fade away like such artifacts of night adaptation often do. It was really there.

And that was not a good thing.

It might only be an apparition. Those happen sometimes, especially in places where there's been the kind of slaughter that had been recorded around Leutenburg. Sometimes they're nothing but echoes, a sort of "recording" of terrible things that have gone before. Sometimes they're souls undergoing their purgation where they were killed.

Sometimes they're of a much worse nature, things of the dark or the abyss itself, drawn by the bloodshed and the horror. Creatures of malice and hunger.

I didn't know which this was, but it was getting closer. It was on my side of the river, too, which was concerning, because I couldn't even hope that the running water might keep it at bay.

It wasn't shaped like a man, or even much of a monster. In fact, I couldn't say that it had much of a shape at all. It was more of a drifting wisp, like a twist of glowing smoke in the dark. But there was a sense of malevolence here that already told me I wasn't dealing with a soul in Purgatory or a mere echo of the violence that had gone before. I'd been to Gettysburg. Seen some strange stuff, but that's all echoes. Reflections of the past. This was very present and very nasty.

Chapter 1

While I couldn't put my finger on it when I drove into town, there was something about Leutenburg that was just a little off.

Now, granted, when you've spent as much time as I have in this profession, you start to realize that every place is a little off. Evil likes to burrow in like a tick, whenever it's given an opening. And human nature being what it is, somebody's always going to open that door. Demons are legalistic, and once they're given a foothold, they'll cling to it by right like the miserliest miser who ever went to sleep holding onto bags of cash.

That metaphor got away from me a little, but you get the idea. The point is, no matter how bucolic and peaceful a place looks on the surface, somewhere there's a dark side to it. Nature of the world as it is.

Of course, the Otherworld is every bit as tenacious in the legalistic department, even if they aren't usually quite as bad as the demons.

I paused at the first of the three stop lights on Main Street, thankful for the momentary red light so that I could take stock. Try to figure out what I'd sensed. I'd gotten hunches before. When you've been on the spooky side of the tracks for long enough, you learn to listen to those hunches.

What's going on isn't necessarily always obvious to the naked eye.

And I'd been on the spooky side of the tracks for a *long* time.

I scanned the street again, looking for whatever might have struck me as Otherworldly. Fr. O'Neill had once called the Otherworld *the world that's just out of sight*, but every once in a while, you could catch a glimpse, especially when the Otherworlders are being cocky or sloppy.

Or when they're hunting *you*.

I was just passing through, heading home to Eryn after investigating what might have been a cult, but had turned out to be nothing more than some dumb kids playing with fire. Eryn hadn't come with me because she was due with our first kid in about four more months. I hadn't heard about anything happening in Leutenberg that required the expertise of a Witch Hunter. In fact, I don't think I had even heard of the town before about half an hour ago, when I saw the sign on the highway.

So, what had I stumbled on?

Nothing caught my attention. Whatever was going on, it wasn't going to be obvious on the surface. It never was.

You might ask how I'd picked up on it, if it was so hidden. I don't know. Maybe my guardian angel gave me a nudge. He does that sometimes. Sometimes he's more subtle than others.

Yes, he's quite real. I've actually met him. He doesn't show up very often, but when he does, it's usually a good sign that things have gone *very* sideways. He wasn't showing up right then, but that didn't mean things *weren't* about to get weird.

Main Street was only two lanes wide, lined with parked cars and trucks. The buildings along either side were mostly old, brick, two-story shopfronts from the late 1800s, early 1900s. Several more modern buildings, including what looked like a four-story condo, stood behind, closer to the hills along the west side of town, but most of the city looked like it hadn't changed much since the '80s. I was pretty well off the beaten track. Ray's ranch, where Eryn and I had made our home, was pretty well out in the boonies, so that was going to happen.

There were about a dozen streetlights every few yards along the sidewalks; the old, sculpted kind with the spherical lampshades. They were already lit, as the sun was going down and the clouds were getting thicker in the north. Several of the storefronts, especially the diner down the street, still glowed, but given what time it was, I was surprised to see how many were already turning the lights out.

The light turned green, and I eased my truck back into motion, rolling down Main Street toward the low motel at the far end of downtown. I didn't move very quickly, just easily cruising down the street in the lack of traffic, taking the opportunity to watch the locals and the rest of the town.

I was getting looks. They were hard to read, in no small part because it was getting dark. But I got the distinct impression that I was being watched with a combination of nervousness and… pity?

That didn't bode well.

Still, I wasn't worried about the locals. Maybe I was getting cocky in my old age, or maybe I'd just seen too much from the darker side of the veil. Sure, ordinary people could still be a threat, but I wasn't getting the cult zombie feeling that I'd seen before, either. There was something wrong here, but I didn't think the locals were necessarily behind it.

They knew about it, but they weren't going to mob me for it. At least, I didn't think so.

From a viewpoint of pure self-preservation, I probably should have kept rolling. Gotten out of town and gotten back to my family. There was no reason I could see to stay, and the heebie-jeebies were usually a warning, not an invitation.

But I'd been on the road for a long time already, and I was hungry. At the very least, I needed to stop, stretch my legs, and get some chow. So, I pulled my truck into the parking lot of the little diner just past the last stoplight, parked, checked that my old 1911 was covered by my jacket, and got out.

It was getting late, and the diner was probably going to close soon. Instinctively, I checked the place out as I walked toward the door, scanning the interior through the big picture windows. There were still about half a dozen people inside, seated at widely separated tables. None of them were watching the door, though every head turned as I walked in.

While I could have sworn that a few of those looks held the same combination of suspicion and pity that I'd seen on main street, after a moment they all turned away, except for the waitress, who seemed awfully nervous as she came up to my table.

Now, I've never been what might be considered harmless looking. I'm tall and raw boned, with deep set eyes and a beak of a nose that's been broken a couple times and that I've never much liked, myself. I don't necessarily get a haircut or a shave all that often, or even eat with the kind of regularity that keeps me filled out. So, I wasn't that surprised that she was nervous, despite the ring on my left hand.

"We're gonna be closing up soon, mister." She didn't quite look straight at me while she spoke, tapping the pen in her hand against her order pad.

I had to raise an eyebrow at that, while I leaned forward on the table. "Seems a little early to be closing. Does this town *really* roll the sidewalks up at sunset, or something?"

She still looked nervous, glancing over her shoulder toward the back of the restaurant, and still avoiding looking me in the eye. "It's just not very busy around here, so we close up early."

There was definitely something wrong here, and I followed her gaze toward the back, though all I could see was the door leading into the kitchen. I shifted my eyes toward the other clientele, but while I caught a couple of furtive looks, quickly turned away as they saw me looking at them, there was nothing that presented an immediate threat.

None of the other folks there in the diner seemed to be in a hurry to finish up. The lights were all still on. The sense of disquiet I'd felt since rolling into town intensified a couple notches.

"I'm mighty hungry, so I promise I won't dawdle over my food." I was hesitant to come right out and ask her what was wrong. My protective streak made me want to, but I hadn't survived as long as I had walking through the shadowy parts of the world without a healthy dose of caution when I couldn't see all the cards. The Otherworld is sneaky, and the demons of the Abyss are worse. "Sure you can't stay open for an extra thirty minutes? It's not *that* late."

She looked over her shoulder again, taking half a step back toward the kitchen. I was watching the shadows. It was entirely possible that I was barking up the wrong tree. There might still be something wrong, but it might just be the regular, homegrown crime sort of wrong. There were small towns like this one that were run like mafia front companies. They were usually somewhere down in the Southwest, but every once in a while, you might find one up here in the mountain states, my usual stomping grounds.

I couldn't be sure, though, so I watched to see if the shadows moved.

"I'll go ask." It sounded like a temporizing measure, but I couldn't really object. She was the waitress, after all. She didn't run the place.

She disappeared into the back, and kept my eyes and my ears open, all without making it obvious that I was keeping tabs on the other diners. They were all studiously ignoring me. Either they had other ways of watching, or they were really trying to mind their own business.

A few minutes later, as the sheriff's SUV pulled up outside, I figured it was probably the latter.

Chapter 2

I wasn't sure at first whether the older man who came through the door was the sheriff or one of his deputies. He was probably in his late fifties, balding, and with a bit of a gut, though I wouldn't have called him fat. He was wearing a uniform jacket over his dark brown shirt, pulled aside to show the star on his chest and hiked up to keep his sidearm clear.

He walked past my table as I leaned back, clearing my access to my own sidearm, just in case. I wasn't eager to get in a gunfight with the local law, but I'd seen enough in little towns where the heebie-jeebies put my hackles up to know that I couldn't necessarily count on things to stay sane. I didn't know what was going on here, but the fact that the diner's staff had apparently called the sheriff over some stranger who just wanted to eat given the relatively early hour didn't bode well at all.

I was taking care not to stare at the sheriff or the waitress as she came to the counter and spoke softly to him, pointing toward my table, of course. The sheriff—his presence and demeanor was making me suspect that he was the sheriff and not just a deputy, though I still couldn't be entirely sure—turned to look at me, then patted the waitress's hand and started toward my table.

I looked up at him as he approached. I'd already put my hands on the table, though I knew I could get to my 1911 fast even so. I just didn't want to start something if I could talk my way out of it.

Right then, I was really wishing that I'd just stayed in the truck and kept on rolling. Something told me that I'd stopped here in Leutenburg for a reason, though.

He stopped just beyond the corner of the table, his thumbs in his belt, one hand noticeably closer to his sidearm, and eyed me. The nametag on his jacket read "Deace." "You were asked to leave, Mister."

I looked up at him, then nodded toward the other clientele, most of whom were turned away, pointedly ignoring our little byplay. "They weren't. It's not even seven o'clock yet, and the sign out front says this place is open until nine." I watched him without blinking. "I haven't done anything, haven't threatened or harassed anyone. I just want to eat a meal in peace."

Something flickered behind his eyes. Was it anger? Or fear? I couldn't tell. He glanced over his shoulder, shifting his weight, clearly uncomfortable. My eyes narrowed slightly as I watched him, my hands still on the table. There was something very, very wrong here.

His eyes returned to me, studying me a little more closely, and then they stopped. I didn't look down to see what he was looking at, but from what I could tell, he was staring at the silver crucifix on its leather thong around my neck.

I'd never try to hide it, though I did occasionally tuck it away inside my shirt when I needed to move. Most people just thought it was jewelry, or a sign of my faith.

It definitely was the latter, but it was also my badge of office, in a way.

Sheriff Deace's eyes were fixed on that crucifix for a long moment, before they moved up to me. His expression was still unreadable, but something had changed. I just didn't know whether it was for the better or worse.

"You're going to have to come with me." His hand had shifted closer to his sidearm.

Definitely worse.

"What have I done, Sheriff?" A part of me couldn't just go along with this. Part of that was sheer survival instinct, which the Marine Corps had honed and then years as a Witch Hunter had stropped to a fine edge. I knew that if I went into a jail in a town that had something from the other side in control, I might not make it out.

That was always a possibility, but it was one you tried to stave off as long as possible. Life is a gift, and while we shouldn't be overly attached to this world, we don't get to throw the gift away, either.

"Are you resisting arrest?"

There it was. I could go along or get into a gunfight with the local law in a diner. That wasn't really an option.

Hopefully this hadn't already gone so far south that I wouldn't get a phone call. At least somebody should know what was going on.

Keeping my hands above the table and spread wide, I slid out of my chair and got up. I was taller than the sheriff, though he probably outweighed me by a good thirty pounds. I could probably still put him on the ground, but I really didn't want to.

He stepped back, though he didn't put hands on me, which was a little weird, given what was going on, but I wasn't going to look a gift horse in the mouth. I preceded him out the door, still careful to keep my hands in view, waiting for things to get rough outside.

But all he did was open the back door of his SUV. "Get in."

I did so, surprised that he hadn't searched me. I still had my pistol on my belt, not to mention the flask of holy water in my back pocket. *What is going on here?*

He didn't say a word as he got in the front seat, and I wasn't going to break the silence until I could figure out more of what was going on. The sense of impending doom that had hung over me since I'd slowed down in Leutenburg hadn't lessened at all.

I just wasn't sure how involved the sheriff was.

Leutenburg not being a large town, it didn't take long to get to the county jail. Still without speaking, Sheriff Deace parked the vehicle, got out, and let me out of the back. He pointed toward the door, still in silence, and I walked through, still being careful not to move too fast or let my hand get too close to my .45.

The office inside was small and pretty typical of a rural county sheriff's office. The venetian blinds were half drawn in the windows along two walls, and instead of industrial cubicles, the office was divvied up by actual wood dividers, with clear plastic windows. There were some plants on shelves and a couple of the four desks, though no one else was in there at the moment.

I had been expecting to get ushered down the hall to the jail, so I wasn't quite sure what to do, but I stepped out of the doorway as Sheriff Deace followed me inside.

"Have a seat." The sheriff pointed toward a chair in front of a desk with "Sheriff Deace" on the little placard in front. "I didn't get your name, but we needed to get out of the diner."

I frowned, but did as he said, while he stepped around the desk and sat down. "Jed Horn."

Deace folded his hands and leaned on his elbows. "Well, Mr. Horn, I apologize for the drama, but I assure you that there's a reason for it."

This could get interesting. "I should hope so." Ordinarily, I might be a little more circumspect, but I was tired, hungry, and had just been through a pseudo arrest for no particular reason.

He had the good grace to look somewhat abashed. "I *was* just going to try to get you out of town. Or, if you put up a fuss, yeah, I was going to throw you in the clink until morning, but…" He held up a hand as my face clouded. "It was for your own protection. You might not buy that right off the bat, but just hear me out."

Then he pointed to the crucifix around my neck. "Then I saw that."

I just raised an eyebrow. I wasn't going to say a thing until I had more information.

"Now, I know it might just be an ordinary cross, but here's the thing. Back when I was a youngster, when we were having the same troubles we are now, a fella came through wearing that same crucifix." He nodded when my eyebrow went up a little higher. "Oh, yeah. I'm certain that it's the same one. I've seen the photos. We've got a few in the files here.

"The point is, this gent was able to help out where no one else could. I'm hoping that maybe that ain't just a piece of jewelry, and you're like him."

Well, this was getting interesting.

"Did he carry a gun?"

"Several, actually." Deace leaned back in his seat with a creak, apparently satisfied enough to relax. I still hadn't been searched, which lent some credence to this not being a trap. "Among other things. Including a hip flask full of holy water."

I sighed. Well, that was a pretty good indicator that another member of the Order had come through here. Still moving carefully, I reached back and pulled my own flask out of my pocket and set it on the desk.

You'd think I'd just produced the Holy Grail. The confirmation that I was, indeed, a member of the Order of the Silver Cross made him slump with a deep sigh of relief.

"What kind of trouble do you think I can help with, Sheriff?" I still wasn't all that happy about how this had gone down, but sometimes there's only so much you can do.

He sobered, leaning forward over the desk again. "So, with anyone else, I'd expect you to think this sounds crazy. But from what I read in the notes from the last time, I hope that you'll hear me out."

I just held my peace. We'd definitely gotten off to the wrong start, but when I swallowed my anger at the way I'd been treated, I had to suspect that some of the bad feeling I'd had when I'd first rolled into town might be explained in the next few minutes.

"So, this town goes back to the 1890s. Founded in 1893, as a matter of fact. And this problem, judging by the town wisdom and records going back to the first newspaper, which was started in 1894, goes right back to the beginning.

"Sam Witwer was the first victim. Sam was the town drunk, so nobody missed him at first. Only when he started to be found around town, in pieces, did anyone really start to take notice. Still, they figured that Sam had finally drunk himself to death, and the coyotes were picking him apart.

"Then it happened again. Only Mary Tannen wasn't a drunk. And her parts and pieces started showing up in almost the exact same places where Sam's limbs had been deposited."

My eyes were narrowing as I listened. This could be any number of things—including ordinary crime—but if he was talking about things that had happened in the 1890s, then I was already starting to think that it was up my alley.

Oh, joy.

See, what the Order does is fight back when the Otherworld and the Abyss try to cheat. The demons of the Abyss will sometimes try to terrify their targets into corruption by force. The Otherworld does the same thing, though for somewhat different reasons. That's not the way the rules work, and that's why we step in, with iron, silver, lead, steel, prayer, and holy water when that happens. We sometimes get some pretty high-level assistance, if you catch my meaning, but we are the front line when things get physical.

"Two more died before they caught the culprit. Matthew Harmon was caught with about half of what was left of Olivia Reitmeier's body. He was covered in blood, dragged in front of the justice of the peace, tried, found guilty in about half an hour, and hanged.

"The really freaky part of the newspaper story was that Harmon didn't even try to deny any of it, and he *laughed* on the way to the tree where they strung him up."

Deace's eyes had drifted to somewhere far away while he'd talked. From the sounds of things, this had been over a century ago, but for some reason the story was deeply affecting him.

Given what he'd said about "current troubles…"

"That was in 1894. About 1912, it happened again. Almost blow for blow. Four victims that time, before Simon

Arendt was caught. Once again, he was tried, didn't even try to deny it, laughed all the way to the gallows."

The sheriff looked haunted as he waved his hand at the stack of papers on his desk. Now that I noticed, I saw that some of them appeared to be very old. "So it's gone. Over and over, for over a hundred years. Every ten to fifteen years, it starts again. And it started again six weeks ago."

I frowned as I thought it over. There were some missing pieces here. "You said one of my order came through here."

He nodded, pulling out a much newer, but still yellowed notebook. "It was the last time. He seemed to think that this was the work of a cult, one that had been around since the town was founded, if not before. He found a ceremonial…something, out in the hills to the north of here and destroyed it. Said he thought they had been trying to summon something, but with the ceremonial site destroyed, they should move on somewhere else. The perp was caught the next day, and the usual song and dance went down. This being the modern day, there wasn't a quick trial or sentencing, but the perp was found dead in his cell after a week. Looked like he'd been beaten to death. There were some questions about how that had happened, but it was essentially over after that."

I thought it over. "But now it's started again?"

He nodded. "Three victims so far. I'm guessing that whatever the other guy did, he didn't put enough of a damper on the cult's activities. Or he really miscalculated."

Without knowing who it was, I couldn't comment on his professionalism, but I'd seen the latter before. That's actually a common risk in this business. Neither the Otherworld nor the Abyss are particularly aboveboard or honest, and half the job is trying to figure out just what is going on. And you can always be wrong, because the beings we deal with are far more cunning than any ordinary man.

"I'd guess that he miscalculated." I was still thinking through what he'd told me, and some of the picture was coming together. I'd have to do some looking around, get on the hunt, but I could make some guesses. My eyes narrowed as I thought it over. "The pattern is too long-lived to just be a cult. And the perp always laughing on the way to the hanging tree…" My frown deepened. "No, I think that if there was a summoning involved, it happened a long time ago. This isn't a ritual. It's a predator."

He'd blanched as I'd spoken. I suppose it's a lot worse to hear that there's some sort of supernatural predator prowling around your jurisdiction, rather than a cult of serial killers. "That's my theory, anyway. I'd have to investigate to tell for sure." My gaze sharpened as I shifted all my attention to him. "Can I do that without running afoul of the locals?"

He had the good grace to look abashed. "Look, I'm sorry for how this started out. But you've got to understand. All the victims lately have been out-of-towners, people passing through or visiting. That was why Mable tried to get you out before dark, and why she called me. She wasn't trying to be hostile. She might not have handled it all that well, but she didn't want to see your body parts show up scattered around the town tomorrow."

I had to nod. Had to accept it, as bitter as I might still have been. My profession might call me to a higher moral level—being in a state of sin makes you vulnerable to some of the things we fight—but I'm still a former Marine with a short temper. It makes things tough, sometimes.

Standing up, I stretched. "Well, then, I guess I'll find a place to bed down and start looking around." I raised an eyebrow as he stood up on the other side of the desk. "Though I'd really like a meal first."

Deace sighed and pulled his jacket off his chair. "Come on. I'll buy."

Chapter 3

I'd decided not to try to stay in the motel in town. I'd already gotten enough looks just going to the diner, though showing back up with Sheriff Deace had helped. He'd still been nervous about the possibility of me staying in town, though with more context, I knew that he was afraid that I was going to show up in pieces the next morning.

It wouldn't necessarily be that easy, but I was more comfortable camping out down by the river anyway.

The evening was cool and quiet, the faint whisper of the wind in the treetops along the river bottoms being the only sounds except for a handful of birds. I sat on my truck's tailgate, having just finished evening prayer, listening and thinking.

Being so still let me hear the movement before I could even see it in the dying light of day. I snapped my .45 up and pointed it, so that as soon as Mickey popped his head up over the tailgate, he found himself staring down the muzzle.

I'd always thought that Mickey looked a lot like Victor McLaglen, though in miniature. He certainly didn't look like the typical image of a leprechaun, but often the Otherworld tends not to work the way we'd expect. I didn't know why, but Mickey looked that way because he *wanted* to.

The creatures of the Otherworld are often nebulous and slippery, and Mickey was no exception.

He froze as soon as he registered that he was staring down the barrel of my hand cannon. "Is that any way to greet an old friend?"

"Considering the nature of your usual 'greetings,' Mickey, yes." I'd been awakened more than once by one of those tiny fists slamming into my ribs. Leprechauns are mischief makers, no matter how reformed they might be. Mickey was generally on the side of the angels, but he sure wasn't one himself.

"Ye wound me, Jedediah." He relaxed slightly as he climbed onto the tailgate and leaned against the side of the bed. "Ye'd think I was going to betray ye to the demons or something." His brogue, I was pretty sure, was as artificial as his appearance, but it was also consistent. Maybe when he'd decided to convert, his affectations had become locked in, deception no longer as easy. I didn't really know, and doubted I'd get a straight answer if I asked.

"I'm just being careful." I tilted my head toward the deepening darkness of the evening. I was willing to put my pistol down, but not to take my eyes off the leprechaun. Few of his kind could stand to wear the cross that he wore around his neck, but still. "Considering there's something nasty prowling around here."

Any pretense of joviality dropped from Mickey's demeanor, and he got deadly serious. "Aye, that's why I came to see ye." He looked around almost furtively.

"You know what it is?"

He shook his head. "No. That I don't, and that I won't be finding out. Not even for ye. Whatever it is, it's old, it's dangerous, and none of my kin are hanging around here.

Were it no that I count ye a friend, I'd not be found around here for love or money."

Well, that was ominous. Mickey had done some reconnaissance for me in the past, and he was as close to fearless of any of his kind that I'd ever run across. That he was this scared did not bode well.

He'd even scouted down a shadowman for me once. That this was worse...

"So, it is a predator."

"That would be putting it mildly." He looked out at the dark and seemed to shiver. It might have been an act, but while Otherworlders such as leprechauns are hard to read, somehow I didn't think so. Whatever was here in Leutenburg, it had *Mickey* rattled. "Look after yerself, Jedediah, because I shan't be here to watch yer back."

And with that, even while I was looking right at him, he was gone.

An owl hooted somewhere down the river, as the shadows grew darker.

I crossed myself again before I crawled into my bivy in the back of my truck, hoping that I could get some sleep before the preternatural killer came looking for me.

***

Sometime during the night, I woke up. Staying still, I opened my eyes to see the stars overhead, a few scudding clouds moving rapidly across the sky. I didn't know what had awakened me, but I'd learned a long time ago never to take such an awakening for granted. Some of that went all the way back to the Marine Corps, and all the time I'd spent in the field. If something wakes you up in the middle of the night, when you're not on security, it might just be a threat. So, instead of cussing, rolling over, and trying to go back to sleep, I lay there and tried to analyze my surroundings.

The wind had picked up and was hissing through the treetops down by the river, though not so loudly as to drown out the gurgle of the water. For a long time, those were the only sounds.

Then I thought I heard something. A cry, somewhere in the distance. It might have been an owl—there are some that don't make the traditional hoot—but there was something about it that didn't sound right.

Now, being a Witch Hunter doesn't lend us any preternatural senses. Sometimes we can rely on our gut instinct, but what any exorcist will tell you is that you've got to be very careful not to attribute everything to demons. Or Otherworldly monsters or tricksters. I still remained motionless, except to cross myself and then reach one hand out to lay it on my old Winchester 86, just in case, and listened.

The cry wasn't repeated. Eventually, I drifted off to sleep again.

***

Dawn came without an attack or any other manifestation. I'd been in some places where the nearness of the monsters tended to either draw other things, or warp reality enough that stuff got weird fast. That didn't seem to be happening here, which was both a relief and a source of worry.

Without those manifestations, this thing could be very hard to hunt.

I got up, said morning prayers, and then sat on my tailgate again, watching the trees in the river bottom and thinking through a plan of action. I'd gotten the locations where most of the remains had showed up from Deace the night before, so that seemed like a good place to start. Without more extensive knowledge of the town—including history that wouldn't necessarily be found in the local newspaper's archives—I couldn't do much else.

So, I packed things up, keeping my weapons handy in the cab, and headed for the first spot. Though not without a prayer that I wasn't going to run into this thing before I was prepared.

Chapter 4

The first of the latest set of gruesome trophies had been found just outside the local cemetery. That seemed to be a reasonable enough place for something like this to hang out, though in retrospect, it wasn't necessarily as clear cut as it might seem on the surface. Whatever this thing was, it was no ordinary ghoul. Not that there's any such thing as an "ordinary" ghoul, as the creatures of the Otherworld aren't like regular people or even animals. We tend to categorize them for our own sense of order and neatness, but no two creatures of the shadows are entirely alike.

That said, Mickey wouldn't have been terrified of an ordinary ghoul.

The cemetery was set on a hill above the rest of the town. Leutenburg wasn't large, main street and most of the businesses being nestled in a narrow valley between bluffs, with some scattered timber on the hillsides that gave way to bunch grass and sagebrush up on the tableland. There weren't a lot of places for something to hide, at least not at first glance.

A few trees had been planted around the fence of the cemetery, though they were all tilted and twisted by the winds that howled along the high ground in this part of the country. At least they all still had their leaves, because I could only imagine how much like grasping, skeletal hands they might have looked during the fall and winter.

Just because I work on the spooky side of the tracks doesn't mean I don't occasionally get spooked. None of this stuff is the sort of thing you ever get *used* to.

I parked outside the gate, made sure my .45 was secure in its holster and my flask of holy water was still in my back pocket, and started to walk around the fence. The wind was picking up, though it wasn't that cold, given the time of year.

The wind rippled in the grass, and everywhere I looked, I thought I could see movement out of the corner of my eye. Already tuned up to look for the monsters, that wasn't helping my frame of mind. I was going to get jumpy if this kept going.

The spot where the body parts—a leg this latest time, though Deace had told me that it had been a head the previous cycle—was on the far side of the cemetery from the gate. I kept scanning my surroundings as I went. Even the monsters can't usually materialize out of thin air, and there weren't many places for anything of any size to hide.

I was well aware just how small a space it took to hide even a grown man. Most people don't understand that it really doesn't take that much. The Apaches and other Indians were masters of popping out of what looked like empty, open ground, because they understood how to use microterrain.

The monsters are even better at it. Which is why I'd gotten good at watching those spots carefully.

I rounded the corner of the fence and slowed down even more, carefully studying the ground. I was looking for tracks, sure. Even Otherworlders tend to leave some trace of their passage, even if it's not a footprint. As I'd feared, though, the grass and the parade of crime scene investigators and gawkers had long since rendered any such marks illegible.

That wasn't all I had to work with, though. If these killings were ritual in nature—and the consistent deposits of body parts in all the same places suggested that they might be—then the thing responsible might have left other marks, things not so easily picked out.

The site where the parts had been left was still fenced off with police tape, tied to the fence and then staked in. I circled wide around it, searching the ground as I went.

There. I stopped dead, squatting down to get a better look.

It was a track, all right. A deep one, as if made by someone heavy, or carrying something heavy. It wasn't one of Sheriff Deace's or anyone else who had been milling around the crime scene, either. I'd made a pretty thorough mental catalog of those tracks, and this didn't match any of them.

It was human, or at least human shaped, but when I looked up in the direction from which it had come, there were no other tracks. No one had gone out that way and come back. Still, I started to backtrack. It wasn't a smoking gun. A taloned, splayed track of obviously monstrous origin would have been more helpful, but the monsters aren't usually interested in being helpful.

Though between Deace's story about the culprit laughing all the way to the gallows and the way Mickey had talked, this one might not care about being evasive, either.

The stories suggested to me that if this was a singular predator, then it couldn't be easily killed. Why else would it laugh on the way to execution?

Unless…

Cases of full-fledged demonic possession are rare. Cases where the demon uses the victim's body to commit heinous crimes like this are even rarer. There are pretty strict limits on what the demons are allowed to do, even as they do their damnedest—pun not intended—to tear men and women away from God.

I backtracked the prints for a few more yards, then took a knee again and studied the rolling ground ahead while I thought things over. There were other possibilities, though they weren't certain, and I wasn't even sure I could buy into some of them.

It was possible that a mortal man had made those tracks. Or it might have been the Otherworldly predator, that was simply shaped like a man. They weren't all mounds of tentacles or teeth with a hundred eyes. At least not all the time. Some of them could look very much like ordinary men and women.

I came back to the idea that it really was an ordinary man. Mind control wasn't a common thing, even when dealing with sorcery and the Otherworld, but it did happen occasionally. It was also conceivable that the monster had a following. You'd be surprised the sorts of things that gathered cults around them, even in otherwise wholesome pockets of Americana like Leutenburg. It might be lying low and letting its cultists do the heavy lifting.

That didn't match up with the laughter of the doomed, though. Or did it? Were they so brainwashed by that point that they were perfectly willing to sacrifice themselves to their chthonic god?

I needed to know more. I crossed myself, lifted my silver crucifix to my lips and kissed it, then got up and moved deeper into the open country, following the footprints.

There's always risk involved in delving too deeply into these things. The monsters are clever, far more so than most humans, and the demons are of another order entirely. Some of them *want* you to get curious, either so they can lure you in and eat you, or—in the case of the demons for the most part—so they can corrupt you.

It's a dangerous line of work in more than one way.

The tracks kept going over the low rise in front of me, and I shifted wide to avoid going over that same rise on the same line. That was an advisable tactic even dealing with ordinary people. Anyone who might expect that they were being followed might set in an ambush in the low ground ahead.

Sure, the prints were all pointing toward the cemetery, but taking anything for granted was probably a bad idea, especially since the locals were worried about outsiders getting murdered.

Keeping low, I worked my way over the rise and toward the small depression on the other side. The ground was getting rocky again, and the depression was deeper than I'd initially thought. Dark, angular basalt outcroppings formed the north and south edges of the depression, and most of the bottom was covered in scattered, broken rock. It was a hole punched in the rolling sagebrush.

Granted, I'd seen places like it before. It wasn't necessarily unnatural. But this close to where the body parts of slaughtered victims had been left, it still made the hair stand up on my arms.

There was something about that pit that bothered me. The shadows inside seemed a little too deep for the time of day. It was warm enough, but I thought I felt a faint chill.

The trail had disappeared into the rocks where the tracks came up out of that hole. I began to circle around the depression, looking for tracks leading in.

By the time I got all the way around, back to where the tracks came out and headed over the rise toward the cemetery, I was starting to hope that I'd missed something.

Because I hadn't seen any tracks going into the depression.

For a couple of minutes, I stood at the edge of the hole, looking around at the grassland and sagebrush around me, listening to the wind whispering over the ground, and the slightly muffled grumble of cars and trucks from Leutenburg over the hill. Nothing moved but the grass, and I couldn't hear anything like the cry that had awoken me the night before.

Looking back down into the hole, I took a deep breath, and then stopped. I sniffed the air again.

Sorcery has a particular scent. It's hard to describe, but it's faintly metallic, redolent of something like burned blood. For a second, I'd thought I'd smelled it.

I could only sigh. My hopes that this might have just been a cult were dwindling. Not that they'd ever been that high to begin with.

Drawing my .45 and letting my silver crucifix hang outside my shirt, I started down into the depression.

The tracks *were* somewhat visible, though only in the shape of disturbed rocks. Tracking isn't just about recognizing full footprints. Most of the time a tracker is just spotting little marks of disturbed earth, bent vegetation, transferred dirt or moisture. Once the track is identified, it's a matter of finding all the little indicators to lead one to the quarry—or where the quarry came from.

And this track led me to the latter.

The thing that had crouched in the middle of the depression had been big. Big and heavy.

A slab of rock had slid down from the outcropping to the north and lay at the bottom of the depression. The thing had crouched on it, leaving marks despite the fact that it takes a lot to mark basalt. White scars had been dug in the rock by claws—at least, I assumed they were claws.

There were also six of them per foot.

The claw marks weren't the only signs left behind. The thing had dripped something on the rock, a dark, tarlike substance that looked a little familiar, though I wasn't going to touch it to make sure.

I looked up at the rim of the depression and the sky above, which was still clear, but suddenly felt darker than it had before I'd descended into the hole in the ground. If I'd been looking for confirmation that this was a monster involved, and one of the more evil ones, then I'd sure found it.

I wasn't any closer to finding out what it was or how to kill or banish it, but it was a start.

Carefully studying every inch of the rocks, I looked for any other indicators. Sometimes things from the Otherworld are proud enough that they want to leave their mark, effectively preternatural graffiti. This thing's actions so far suggested that it might just be that arrogant.

I saw nothing, though. No sigils, no glyphs, no eldritch name scrawled in blood or whatever that tarlike substance was. It might be cocky, but it wasn't stupid enough to give that sort of a clue.

That might be a clue in and of itself. If concealing its true identity was key to its apparent immortality, then I might have a thread to try to pull on.

If I could find it without getting my head ripped off.

Finally deciding that I wasn't going to find any more actionable intel in that hole, I was eager to get out. I started to clamber back out the way I'd come, my boots slipping in the scree a little bit until I was back up onto the grass.

It was noticeably warmer up there, which was another sign.

I started to circle back around the cemetery, heading for my truck, still scanning and thinking. I had a bit more information, but I still didn't have any good idea of where this thing might go to ground. Presuming that it *did* go to ground.

The claw marks and the footprints raised some more questions. There might still be a cult involved. If the monster had made the claw marks, and had sent its lackey to deposit the remains…

But that just raised more questions. Where had the cultist gone? There were no return prints going back to the rock where the monster had crouched.

Fortunately, I'd sort of gotten used to this part of the job. Hunting the creatures that lurk just out of sight is never straightforward or easy. I'd have to keep my eyes and ears open as I roamed around Leutenburg, with the understanding that I was the hunted as much as I was the hunter.

Also fortunately, I had some pretty heavy-duty backup. It just wasn't the sort that could be seen most of the time.

The Otherworld and the things that really were their masters—despite what some of the more powerful creatures wanted to believe—often had a lot more sound and fury, but less actual power. It was a difficult thing to wrap one's head around sometimes, but necessary.

The Enemy will try to frighten you off or overawe you into bending the knee. It becomes a balancing act to make sure that you don't buy into the spook show, while also not getting so overconfident that you end up playing into the hands of creatures immensely older, more powerful, and more cunning than any ordinary human being. It was a tightrope that I had seen some fail spectacularly, in both directions.

As I walked down along the fence, I saw that I wasn't alone anymore. Someone had pulled up in an SUV that looked like it cost three times as much as my truck, and I wasn't driving the old F100 anymore.

A small man was standing in front of the closed gate to the cemetery, his hands clasped behind his back, his head bowed. I couldn't hear over the wind—between the Marine Corps and a few fights afterward without earpro, my hearing ain't what it once was—but he might have been praying, or chanting.

He turned, startled, as I came around the corner, my boot scraping on the gravel. He really must have been absorbed in his prayer not to have noticed me as I walked down the hill. The trees were placed fairly evenly around the fence, but not so thickly that I could have hidden from him.

The man was young, probably in his early thirties, clean shaven and with longish hair. There was a softness about him that suggested he hadn't done much hard work, at least not the kind I'd call hard work. His clothes were simple but on closer inspection, very expensive. This guy had money. Of course, the Escalade behind him had already told me that.

"Oh. Hello." He unclasped his hands, which was when I noticed that his fingers had been intertwined strangely. Almost as if he'd been trying to create a symbol with his hands.

Maybe it was nothing. Maybe I was just jumpy, now that I was on the track of an Otherworldly killer that apparently could be hanged and not die. I didn't react, didn't even look that closely. I just filed it away in my mental intel folder until I found out more.

Again, this is rarely an up-front sort of job.

"I'm sorry, I didn't see you coming." He seemed nervous, and he wasn't looking me in the eye, which was a little strange. I mean, I know I'm tall, rawboned, and not particularly pretty at the best of times, but it always throws me a little when people act like I'm intimidating. "I know, I should have guessed you'd be around when I saw your truck, but, well..." He just kind of trailed off.

"Hey, it's a public place." I was admittedly getting a little uncomfortable with his nervousness. I couldn't say why, but there was something off about this situation. "Sorry if I interrupted you. Were you praying for somebody buried here?"

I don't know exactly why I asked that question, but maybe my guardian angel prodded me.

He does that from time to time.

The young man blinked. "Uh. Not really. Um. Sorry. I wasn't expecting anyone to be here." He swallowed. "Uh, you're the stranger that got the sheriff called on him in the Coal Bucket Diner, right?"

My suspicions were getting a little elevated, and when he changed the subject like that, I really started to pay more attention. "Seems like everybody in town knows about that already." Not that I'd been mixing much since the night before, but it was a small town, and that I should meet a rando at the cemetery who had heard about it suggested that word really did travel fast. "You live around here?"

"I have a place here." As if I needed another indicator that this guy was loaded. *So, what's he doing hanging around the cemetery at the same time I'm looking over where the last set of body parts got left?* "I bought it last year." He shrugged with a faint smile. "I'll admit that part of my interest was the story of the Leutenburg killer. I wasn't expecting to be here when the next… iteration began."

He was holding something back. For the moment, that was fine. So was I. I wasn't the sheriff, and unless this guy turned out to be a cultist, he wasn't my concern.

Granted, there were already a few warning signs, but I just mentally cataloged them for later.

"I'll admit, I'm surprised you're still here," the young man said, turning to face me. He actually looked me in the eye now, seeming to relax as I let his change of subject go unchallenged. "Most people who have gotten 'the talk' from Sheriff Deace left that night."

"Well, as it happens, I have some experience that the sheriff thought might be helpful. So, I'm sticking around." I wasn't going to say much more than that. Most people aren't ready to find out about the Order in the first place, and a lot of modern folks would absolutely flip their lid if they found out what my official job title is.

"Really?" If anything, he seemed to be more interested. "Like a private investigator?"

"Something like that." I tilted my head to study him. "What, exactly, do you find fascinating about a serial killer that carves his victims up? And then, apparently, inspires a copycat every generation or so?"

Something slammed shut behind his eyes. It was subtle, but I spotted it. I'd just touched a nerve, somehow, and I didn't know how. I'd have to keep an eye on this guy.

Maybe, somehow, he'd lead me to my quarry. Maybe.

The other possibility was that I'd just discovered another wild card in this game.

He caught himself as he reacted and tried to cover it with a smile. "You know. Too many true crime documentaries. Once things started to heat up around here again, I was already a little too committed. It wasn't as if I could sell the place while someone was carving people up around town."

"What brings you out to the cemetery, then?" I wasn't going to let that go, though I still had to be at least a *little* subtle about it. "Doesn't seem like you're hunkering down to wait it out until the killer's caught."

He laughed, though there was a brittleness to it. He didn't want to talk about the cemetery. "Well, I've learned a few things over the years, myself. I'm not working directly for Sheriff Deace, but I think everyone should do what they can to help their community, don't you?" He stuck out his hand. "I'm Harper, by the way."

"Jed." His handshake was about what I'd expected. Kind of limp, soft, and clammy. That wasn't necessarily a tell; I'd known few rich young people who had what I'd consider a respectable handshake. He might just be what he appeared.

But there was something going on with this guy. I found myself hoping that he wasn't going to offer to work together, and trying to think of how to say "No" gracefully.

He didn't ask, though. "Well, I should probably be going. I'll see you around, Jed." There was a faint hint of trepidation when he said that.

Trepidation, and something else. Harper was hiding something. And as I went to my own truck, I started to think that I needed to find out just what that was.

Chapter 5

The sun was going down as I finished my circuit of the town, checking all the places where the victims had been deposited. It was gruesome work, even though the remains had long since been moved. The knowledge of what had happened in those places—multiple times—was still there.

I wasn't going back to my campsite, though. Not right away. I had some local history to learn first.

The large brick building standing on the bluff above the town, almost opposite the cemetery, had drawn my eye since I'd first rolled through. It was obviously abandoned, the windows all broken, staring at the town with gaping dark holes like a dozen eyes. It looked like it had probably been around since the early 20th century, maybe even the late 19th, though if the town only dated back to 1893, then it was probably a little newer than that.

Despite Sheriff Deace's effective sponsorship, few of the locals really wanted to talk to me. They weren't hostile, at least not most of them. For the most part, they seemed to just not want to get too friendly with the guy who was likely to end up a meat jigsaw puzzle in the next week.

I could understand that. It was still a pain, and potentially robbed me of an important source of information, but I could understand.

So, when it became clear that I wasn't really going to be able to ask around and get a straight answer, I headed for the next best choice. The local library.

That might seem like a strange place to go for answers about matters eldritch and threatening, but most small towns have a local library, and most of those libraries, despite the current trends, maintain town records and at least scans of town newspapers, oftentimes going back to the beginning.

I got the same sort of pitying look from the librarian, who might have been eminently datable if I weren't married and considered to be a dead man walking around here. Still, she didn't give me the cold shoulder but showed me to the computer with the scans of the old newspapers. They didn't actually have the papers anymore, at least not where they were accessible.

This was probably easier and more convenient, but I still wasn't all that happy about it. I can think of a lot of things I'd rather do than stare at a computer.

Go wandering into a haunted, abandoned brick building on a hillside in the dark, for instance.

The building, it turned out, was an old sanitarium. I felt myself grimacing as I identified it, and read the story of the fire that had gutted the place in the Thirties, killing at least a dozen people. If ever there was a place that a monster might use as a den, that sure seemed like it might be it.

Of course, that didn't mean that it was anything definite, but it was likely spot.

That also meant it was probably a trap. Something didn't seem quite right about it, as if it was a little *too* perfect a target.

I leaned back in my chair and rubbed my chin. I hadn't had a shave in a couple of weeks. I imagined that some of the pitying looks I was getting were probably because I looked half like a hobo. That tends to happen when I'm on the road hunting down the things that go bump in the night for a while.

Maybe I'm just being paranoid. I shook my head. There's no such thing in this business. Witch Hunters who go wandering into dark places thinking that because they're on the side of the angels, that they can't possibly lose, tend not to last long.

The lucky ones just get killed.

No, you've got to be smarter than your average horror movie protagonist in this business.

The other deposit sites hadn't yielded much more in the way of clues, though I'd found the same claw marks and weird, tarlike drips in a couple of them. Nothing new. Nothing that pointed to where it might hide during the day.

The fact that the claw marks only showed up once in each place bothered me. A shapeshifter? If that was the case, then things were really going to get weird and dangerous, quickly. Especially if it was one that was this hard to kill.

So, I'd check the old sanitarium in the morning. It was a possibility, so I had to check it out.

Even in daylight, I couldn't say I was looking forward to it.

***

There were times when I really thought I should get a dog. Dogs are sensitive to the Otherworld, and they make great sentries as a result, even if they're napping.

I hadn't gotten one, though. It was on the list of things that would be nice that I hadn't gotten to. I had to rely on my own instincts—and possibly my guardian angel—to wake me up if things got weird.

Not that things were getting weird every time I woke up in the middle of the night, but I'd gotten into the habit of staying still and listening carefully every time it happened, usually saying a silent prayer to start with. After all, the sort of shadow warfare that was my profession these days involved things that didn't have the same limitations that the insurgents I'd fought in Iraq did. I could be in a place that *should* be secure and safe, but unless I was on holy ground—and even that wasn't always a flawless lock, either—there was no such thing in most places.

It didn't take long, lying there and silently praying the Pater Noster as my hand moved to my 1911, to figure out that something was very wrong.

The whispers weren't immediately noticeable. The wind in the treetops near my campsite, along with the mutter of the river over the rocks, almost drowned them out. They were there, though, and the longer I listened, the clearer they got, all without getting actually louder.

I couldn't make out words, and I quickly realized as I came to full consciousness that I really didn't want to. The malice in the voices was palpable, and I was pretty sure there was more than one.

Sitting up, I had my .45 in my hand. I had a mix of silver and iron loads—I'd used bullets jacketed in those metals before, but they tended to require some machining and tore up barrels pretty quick, so now I had hollow points with BBs of either embedded in the cavities—but right then I wasn't sure if either was going to be useful. The weight of the weapon was still comforting, though.

Spiritual strength is our most potent weapon, and the understanding that we Witch Hunters, by ourselves, can't do squat against the really dangerous things, the ones that come crawling out of the abyss. Even some of the Otherworlders are far beyond us, and only help from on high is going to get us through. But sometimes firearms and knives are still useful tools, and most of us are old gunfighters anyway.

Ain't none of us perfect, or we probably wouldn't be here anymore.

Movement caught my eye, even in the dark, and I shifted my position, making the truck rock a little, to peer out past my truck topper toward the river. Running water could be a deterrent to some of the monsters in the shadows of the Otherworld, but not always, and that was where I'd seen *something*.

For a while, I couldn't see anything but the deeper shadows in the river bottom, while the whispers susurrated and hissed at me. The hair was standing up on the back of my neck. I can't stress enough that my profession doesn't confer any preternatural senses, but I *knew* I wasn't alone down there by the river that night.

Sliding out of the bed of the truck, I shoved my feet into my boots before I dropped to the ground. I stayed in place for a handful of heartbeats, then reached back into the bed and pulled my Winchester to me, holstering the pistol as soon as I had a good grip on it.

I had the rifle loaded the same as the pistol, with alternating silver and iron. The thing about the preternatural is that when it interacts directly with the physical world, that can go both ways. And some Otherworlders have extreme reactions to certain metals, for various symbolic reasons.

"Symbolic" doesn't mean "imaginary."

The whispers changed slightly as I reached under my shirt and drew out my silver crucifix, making sure it hung outside my clothes. Whatever was out there, it didn't like that symbol. That wasn't surprising.

I still couldn't see anything. The trees were dark silhouettes against the stars and the faint light of the sky, and as I looked around, I could start to see a hint of the whitewater through the rocks in the river under the starlight.

Then I saw something that wasn't starlight or reflected starlight.

The eyes can play tricks as much as the mind can, in the dark. Without the amount of light that they're used to, they start to try to fill in details, details that aren't always there. But those illusions are easily dismissed as such once you get another look, even when sleep deprived.

When I looked straight at the smoky light moving along the riverbank, it didn't fade away like such artifacts of night adaptation often do. It was really there.

And that was not a good thing.

It might only be an apparition. Those happen sometimes, especially in places where there's been the kind of slaughter that had been recorded around Leutenburg. Sometimes they're nothing but echoes, a sort of "recording" of terrible things that have gone before. Sometimes they're souls undergoing their purgation where they were killed.

Sometimes they're of a much worse nature, things of the dark or the abyss itself, drawn by the bloodshed and the horror. Creatures of malice and hunger.

I didn't know which this was, but it was getting closer. It was on my side of the river, too, which was concerning, because I couldn't even hope that the running water might keep it at bay.

It wasn't shaped like a man, or even much of a monster. In fact, I couldn't say that it had much of a shape at all. It was more of a drifting wisp, like a twist of glowing smoke in the dark.

But there was a sense of malevolence here that already told me I wasn't dealing with a soul in Purgatory or a mere echo of the violence that had gone before. I'd been to Gettysburg. Seen some strange stuff, but that's all echoes. Reflections of the past. This was very present and very nasty.

I could have taken a shot at it. Sometimes that's enough, even with the more non-corporeal entities. It's not that gunfire can actually damage such a thing, but a four-hundred-five-grain bullet makes for a powerful gesture of rejection.

Something told me, as the thing drifted closer, that while this *might* work, it wasn't an ideal solution. Instead, while I kept my Winchester in my left, I reached up, made the Sign of the Cross, and then put my hand on the crucifix at my neck.

It didn't like that. While it's hard to describe a floating cloud of not much as having reactions, its movements and the general *sense* around it made it seem to recoil. My eyes narrowed as it stopped its forward drift, but it didn't back up.

We could have stood there in a standoff all night, but I was getting mad. I hadn't asked for any of this, and this thing was a scavenger, a parasite feasting on horror, pain, and death.

Furthermore, it had woken me up in the middle of the night. I didn't know what time it was, but I just wanted to go back to sleep.

I took a step forward, still holding up the little silver crucifix, and started a litany of deliverance. It was usually aimed at demonic activity—and it wasn't one that only an exorcist could use; I'm just a layman—but even if this thing was of the Otherworld, it clearly disliked the holy enough that it didn't want to stick around.

After another step, it visibly shrank back. Or maybe it was just shrinking. Without shadows or any real reference points, it was hard to say how big it was, or even quite how close it was.

I was chanting the litany now, my voice low. There was no need to shout it, though I'd known some people who would. The thing shrank back again, then, almost as if it had blinked, it was gone.

I finished the litany. Not because it was magic—superstition only plays into the Enemy's hands—but because I didn't entirely trust that it was gone, and it's just good to finish a prayer once you start it. Otherwise it's like stopping a conversation in the middle of a sentence.

Then, when there was no further sign of my tormentor, I turned back to my truck and crawled back into my sleeping bag.

Something didn't want me around, but I'm not that easy to get rid of.

Chapter 6

The morning was cool, the sky cloudless. I walked down to the river to take a look around, in case my visitor the night before had left a calling card.

It had. There was a withered patch of grass roughly where I remembered the wisp hovering, and it looked like something corrosive had dripped onto the ground in the center.

I already knew that I wasn't going to like what I found, but I had to look. Anything left by a thing like that wasn't going to be good and wasn't something that should be left lying around for just anyone to stumble across, especially in a place like Leutenburg. Nothing it would have left would be good.

I was right. A dollop of brownish substance, that was smoking in the early morning light, had spread into the beginnings of a sigil. I didn't recognize it, but I try not to make a deep study of such symbols. Like the creatures that draw them, they are deceptive, often intended to draw in the curious and get into their heads.

The sigil wasn't the worst part, though. There was a finger bone lying in the center of the puddle of ichor. A finger bone pointing at my truck, and still streaked with blood.

I looked up and around with a grimace. I was going to have to do something about this, but I wasn't looking forward to it. Fortunately, sometimes the right tool for the right job is already at hand.

Pulling out the flask in my back pocket, I unscrewed the top and splashed holy water on the ground in the shape of a cross.

The ichor immediately smoked, bubbled, and melted away where the holy water struck. I could have sworn that I heard a hiss that wasn't the slime boiling away. That thing was still lurking nearby.

Once the last of the sticky, evil stuff was gone, I bent down to pick up the finger bone. It was still streaked with blood, and it looked relatively fresh. I winced a little as I picked it up. There were going to be more body parts on the ground soon. I was almost sure of that.

Why had that thing brought this to me? It had to have been a threat. I didn't think for a moment that the apparition I'd confronted the night before was the predator killing people around Leutenburg. This little deposit told me that it wasn't just a random scavenger from beyond the veil, brought close by the scent of blood, death, and fear, either. No, it had been *sent* after me. Sent to scare me off.

Well, I'd been confronted by a lot worse already. Mobs of goatmen scare me more than a single wisp in the dark leaving unearthly graffiti and bones around.

Carefully burying the bone and saying a prayer over it, I started back up the bank to my truck.

The old sanitarium awaited.

***

The place was harder to get to than I'd expected. There was a road leading up to it, but it wasn't well maintained, and in fact from the weeds growing in the center, I suspected that I was the first to go up there in a long time. That was a clue. I might be barking up the wrong tree.

Or else this thing really was clever, and it was using the locals' reticence to approach the crumbling old building to its advantage.

There was a chain link fence around the place, with a padlocked gate across the weed-choked road. I parked the truck and got out, pausing to consider whether it was worth the trouble to sling my Winchester and take it in. The 1911 would be a lot handier in those close quarters, and climbing the fence with a forty-five-inch-long rifle across my back was not going to be fun.

I wasn't going to try to cut or pick the lock, though I had the tools to do either. I was working here on the sheriff's request and sufferance, and I didn't intend to be a loose cannon about it.

That would be a good way to either get thrown in jail or thrown to the wolves.

Granted, I was still trespassing, but if I could avoid unnecessary property damage along the way, so much the better. The town owned the place, anyway, judging by the sign on the fence, so it wasn't as if I was trespassing on a local's property.

The fence shook and rattled as I climbed over. I wasn't the size I'd been when I'd jumped fences as a kid. It was still easier than climbing a compound wall in Iraq in full gear.

I hit the ground harder than I'd intended, though I wasn't so old that I couldn't bend my knees to cushion the blow. Staying crouched where I was, my hand went to my pistol as I watched and listened to see if anyone—or anything—had noticed me.

The wind sighed through the broken windows and the handful of trees clustered around the old brick building. The center section was three stories high, the roof still mostly white, though turned chipped and dingy over the years. The two wings to either side were only two stories, but seemed even more run down, with a hole in the wall on the right and the roof half caved in on the left.

This place was a death trap even if there was no monster lurking in the dark on the other side of those hollow windows.

An engine sounded close, and I turned to see Sheriff Deace's truck coming up the road behind my own. I sighed. It was daylight, so I should have expected this. I stayed where I was, going back to studying the edifice in front of me.

Deace parked, shut off the engine, and then got out of his truck, slamming the door and raising the echoes from the hills and the brick structure in front of me. "You know, you could have just come to see me, and I would have let you in." He sounded tired and vaguely amused. At least he wasn't mad. He picked up the padlock and started to open it, the rattle of the chain and the fence almost drowning out his words.

I waited until he dragged the gate open to speak. "Didn't want to bother you." I was torn. It was a perfectly normal human reaction to be glad that he was there. I hadn't been looking forward to going into that dark, crumbling ruin by myself. On the other hand, having to look after Deace in an environment he wasn't prepared to deal with was not a pleasant prospect.

Sometimes, as scary as it might be, it was better to go into these places alone. There's no way to really "watch your back," since these things could move right past your face if they wanted to, without you seeing them. They don't necessarily follow the same rules that regular human beings do.

"You're hunting the same thing I am. This is my job." Deace didn't actually sound all that enthused as he walked over to join me and looked up at the forbidding edifice of the old sanitarium. He shook his head. "Man, this place has always given me the creeps. You think our perp is in there?"

I shrugged. The fact was, I was working on instinct and hunches. "Maybe. If it is, it's not the kind of perp you're used to." I waved a hand to indicate the ground around us. I hadn't made a detailed study, but I could see enough to be sure. "No tracks except ours. No one's come in here on foot lately."

I felt him look over at me, while I kept scanning the empty windows. "Maybe we're barking up the wrong tree then?" There was a note of hope in his voice that I hated to dash, but there was no other way.

"Maybe. I doubt it, though." I finally turned and looked at him as I drew my .45. "You might want to stay out here, Sheriff. If I need backup, or need somebody to drag me out of the rubble when a floor or a ceiling collapses on me, I'll yell."

I could see the conflict written on his face. He really didn't want to go in there, but at the same time, he wasn't thrilled with the idea of letting me go in alone. I thought it was a combination of concern for my safety, a sense of duty on his part, and doubts about me. After all, he had kind of hired me based on a hunch. He didn't know anything about me.

Waiting for his response could take a while. So, while I was risking some of the little rapport we'd built, I decided to force the issue. Press-checking my .45, I started toward the weed-choked door, sagging on its hinges.

For a second, I thought he was going to follow me. The long sigh he let out was both resigned and relieved, though.

I half expected the door to fall off its hinges as I pulled it open, but while it scraped on the steps and didn't exactly open smoothly, it still stayed up.

Inside it was dark, despite the sunlight outside. Most of the windows opened onto rooms along the interior, rather than the main entryway and hallway in front of me. Pulling a flashlight out of my pocket, I started inside.

The entryway wasn't as debris-choked as I might have expected. The floors were cracked, the plaster peeling off the walls, and some bits of the ceiling had fallen. There was still detritus against the walls, some of it looking like the remains of animals that had gotten in and not been able to get out. At first glance, it was just an ordinary abandoned building, nothing particularly spectacular.

Something on the far wall drew my eye. The play of light and shadow made it hard to see, but even so, it made my eyes itch. I already had a pretty good idea what it was before I stepped closer.

Sure enough, it was a sigil. One painted on the wall in what looked like blood.

I sighed. It wasn't that terrifying, even though it was the sort of symbol that made your head start to hurt if you looked at it too long. I'd seen these sorts of things far too much to get panicky. They were just the symptoms. Warning signs. And after the apparition of the night before, I kind of suspected that this was another attempt to get rid of me.

The place smelled musty, but there wasn't the sort of stench that I might have expected in a monster's lair. It just smelled like an old, abandoned building.

Even as I thought it, though, I heard something from the north wing, and the temperature abruptly seemed to drop. "Ah, hell."

I still pulled out my flask of holy water and splashed the sign of the cross on the sigil on the wall. It didn't melt away the same way as the one down by the river, but this had been drawn in blood, not ectoplasmic ichor. There was still a faint shudder that might have gone through the building, and I thought I heard a distant snarl.

Turning toward the north wing, I stuffed the holy water flask back in my pocket and put both hands on my pistol. There was no guarantee that whatever had just arrived in the old sanitarium would respond to pistol bullets, but some old habits die hard.

I was pretty sure that whatever it was, it had just arrived. If this had been the killer's den, there should have been more indicators. Sure, I hadn't swept the whole building—I'd only just made entry. But I'd been in places where creatures of the Otherworld had set up shop—creatures that were a lot less nasty than whatever I was hunting here in Leutenburg—and I'd known almost immediately. The signs are there if you know what to look for.

No, I was increasingly convinced that this was a trap. I wondered if my predecessor who had hunted this thing had faced the same sort of situation. The sanitarium, with its appearance and reputation, seemed like a logical place to start, and the sigil in the entryway had probably been placed there to confirm it.

I should just head for the exit. But if there really was something Otherworldly in there—whether it was my quarry or something else—I was now kind of obligated to do something about it.

The hallway leading toward the north wing led past the main stairway that curved upward toward the second floor. That stairwell was even darker than the rest of the interior, and I pivoted to cover it with my .45 as I went by, more out of habit than anything else. Nothing leapt out at me. I heard something fall deeper into the north wing, and again there was that hint of a distant snarl.

There was something back there, all right. Some places, I would have expected a wild animal that had gotten in, like the critters that were half mummified on the floor back in the entryway, but the intensifying cold told me that wasn't the case here.

The north wing was decidedly more run down than most of the rest of the place. There was more debris on the floor, and tiles and plaster had fallen off the walls and the ceiling. A light fixture had fallen and lay in pieces on the floor. I stepped over the worst of the detritus, careful not to get too close to any of the doors that stood open on either side of the hallway.

I was trying to be quiet out of habit more than anything else. Years of hunting on the shadowy side of the veil should have disabused me of the idea that I could sneak around the creatures of the Otherworld, let alone the Abyss, but the Marine Corps had trained me well, and some things you don't just turn off. It's human nature to try to be stealthy when a threat is nearby, and from the sounds coming from the end of the hall, and the last door, there was definitely a threat in here.

There was more clattering and clacking, as if something big was shuffling through the wreckage. It hadn't shown itself yet, but I slowed as I got closer to the end of the hall, my .45 coming up as I searched for the threat.

It must have either heard me or smelled me. Or just decided that right then was the time to reveal itself.

With a screech, it burst out of the east door at the end of the hall, hitting the doorjamb with its shoulder as it came, and skidded on the smashed tiles littering the floor, dropping one taloned hand to the floor to steady itself.

"Oh, hell."

I had to admit that I'd been hoping that it was just a goatman or something. They were nasty, and definitely not natural, but they were manageable. Vicious but dumb, they were Otherworldly thugs, not much more.

This wasn't a goatman.

It was easily seven feet tall if it stood upright. Covered in feathers, it looked vaguely human and female in shape, except for the wings, which were cramped in the narrow hallway, and the enormous, black eyes behind a short, vicious beak. Its hands and feet were taloned like a bird's feet.

I'd never seen a Tah-tah kle-ah before, but I knew what they were.

This was gonna be a fight.

Chapter 7

The owl woman opened her beak and screamed at me, then threw herself down the hall toward me, talons grasping as her wings spread to fill the hallway. Fortunately for me, the hall was too small for those wings, and they actually hindered her.

I already had my .45 in my hand and I fired a snap shot at her as I dove for the nearest door. I had barely tried to aim, being more focused on getting away from those grasping talons and that nasty beak, and the bullet didn't do more than clip some feathers from the wing. It was enough to stagger her, though, as she snatched the wing back and missed a step, giving me a second to get into the room.

Unfortunately, there wasn't any place to go from there except out the window. And while I was pretty sure this was a diversion, I couldn't exactly leave a Tah-tah kle-ah on the loose. I had to deal with this, and I had to do it in here, before she broke out and tore Sheriff Deace to pieces.

In taking cover, though, I'd just reduced my maneuvering options, and that thing knew it.

A taloned hand gripped the doorframe, and the owl-witch lunged into the opening, her black eyes glaring around for me. I shot her again, double tapping an iron and a silver round into her chest. She reared back with another screech and disappeared.

I had no illusions that the pair of bullets had done much. Killing something like a Tah-tah kle-ah takes more than just a couple of rounds, even if they were silver or iron, and I didn't know if the owl witches even had weaknesses to those metals.

Nobody really knew their origin. The tribal stories were kind of vague. Some thought they were once human, others thought they had always been monsters of the Otherworld. The Yakamas had said that they ate snakes and insects, when they weren't kidnapping Indian children and eating them.

What did seem to be agreed was that bullets wouldn't kill them, and that I did *not* want her to touch me. Instant death at contact was unlikely, though some of the legends said that even the brush of a Tah-tah kle-ah's feather would kill.

Many of those stories came from before the missionaries had come. It wasn't certain that my own faith, the silver crucifix at my neck, and the holy water in my pocket was going to save me from that instant death, but there was a good chance. I'd seen it happen before, at least with other monsters.

That didn't mean I was going to take unnecessary chances.

I pied off the doorway, keeping my weapon leveled. I didn't know how much my bullets were actually hurting it, but if they could at least keep it off me for a while, I could get to something that might be able to finish it off.

I just had to stay alive long enough to figure out what that might be.

Contrary to what a few of my compatriots might have said, I don't have an exhaustive encyclopedia of the Otherworld in my head. For one thing, that would generally be completely useless, because the Otherworld doesn't act like a game or some fantasy writer's worldbuilding. As soon as you think you've got a handle on the rules, they change.

The Abyss is worse, but the Otherworld is a lot slipperier than some naïve fools would think.

She was still in the hallway, crouched with her wings tucked back, down on all fours like a more lupine predator, her hind legs thrown out and wide. For all the owl-like features, this was not an owl.

Nor was it a woman. It was a monster, and if I let myself start to think of it as anything else, I was dead.

It was staring at me, its beak agape. If it was going to try to taunt me or say something, but I wasn't there to banter with the monsters. I shot it three times, driving it back with screeches that were barely audible over the bark of my pistol, which was pretty loud and painful in that tiled, dusty hallway, with no real ear protection.

That gave me my opening, and I ducked out of the doorway and ran for the entrance.

Through the ringing deadness in my ears, I heard the creature scrabbling in the shattered tiles on the floor, its weight and its talons cracking more of them, as it came after me.

I'd made it halfway to the entryway when I realized that I wasn't going to make it. I could almost feel the monster's breath on the back of my neck, so I threw myself into the next doorway, twisting around to bring my .45 to bear once more.

This time I shot it in the mouth from point blank range. I was packing nine rounds in the gun, but I'd already shot this thing six times. It still reared back, its wings flapping in a combination of rage and agony as it crashed onto its back. The bullet hadn't had that much of an impact—

it had been the shock and the pain of the wound that had thrown it off.

Scrambling back to my feet, I lunged for entrance again, but it was adapting.

Rather than try to catch me from behind again, the Tah-tah kle-ah threw itself into the air as I tried to get up. I was still pointing my pistol at it, so it didn't come right after me, but it went over my head, skimming the ceiling and coming down with a crash right between me and the way out.

It gaped its beak at me again, as I twisted around, one hand still on the floor, the other still pointing my 1911 at it. It croaked.

"Shot me. No kill. Soon, you die."

That I had heard about these things. That if you shot one but didn't manage to kill it, you'd be the next to die. That sounded like a curse, though, and curses aren't as unavoidable as the things in the dark would have you believe.

It was chanting, though, an ugly, low, croaking and clicking tune that immediately started to make my head hurt. I could feel the pressure mounting, and the metallic stink of burned blood joined the musty smell of the abandoned building.

My hand moved to the crucifix at my neck, lifting it in front of my face. The first words of the deliverance litany came out as a harsh rasp, but the Tah-tah kle-ah recoiled, the chant faltering as I regained my own voice, the Latin syllables rolling down the hall.

It shrieked again, and flew at me, taloned hands spread and grasping for my life.

I shot it three more times, the slide locking back on the empty mag as the impacts made it stagger and drop to all fours again. I ran for the stairwell, dropping the empty out as

I went. Under different circumstances, I'd probably try to retain the mag, but this was a survival situation. If I lived, I could retrieve it later.

The reload passed the empty in midair, and I let the slide slam forward almost the same instant that the mag was fully seated. I could hear the owl witch behind me, clawing her way back to her feet, hissing and squawking.

Salt. The thought came to me as I finished the stanza of the litany, the sound of which seemed to be slowing the Tah-tah kle-ah down. The owl witch might not be a demon of the abyss, but she was clearly of the segment of the Otherworld evil enough that the holy did not agree with them.

I didn't know where I'd heard it, or even when, but somewhere along the line, I'd heard about salt being involved in killing things like this. Blessed and exorcised salt could have a powerful effect in this sort of warfare, comparable to holy water.

Which was why I'd added a coach gun loaded with blessed and exorcised rock salt to the arsenal. Unfortunately, that was still in my truck, next to the Winchester.

I couldn't remember whether there was a side door at the end of the hall. The sanitarium had been built at the turn of the century, so it wasn't guaranteed.

Reaching the stairwell at the end of the hall, I found that most of the stairs had collapsed, choking the opening with debris and denying me an upward escape route. I turned again, my pistol in one hand, scooping the crucifix up again with the other, and faced the oncoming owl witch.

She was moving again, though there was a hesitancy that hadn't been there before. She was moving more slowly, almost as if she was carrying a great weight. My voice got louder as I continued the litany, each word hammering at the creature like a physical blow.

I held my fire, since I was mainly looking for a way out at that point. Shooting it again with the .45 wasn't going to do much except piss it off even more and might—depending on a number of unquantifiable factors—even give it more of an opening. It was starting to croak its own chant again, trying to counter the litany with its curse.

Then Deace did the one thing I'd hoped he wouldn't.

"Horn? You all right?"

The owl witch didn't immediately turn toward him, but glared at me, with a new degree of malevolence in its black-eyed stare. Its beak gaped again, and I knew that things were about to turn from bad to worse.

"Deace, get out of here!" I brought my .45 up, knowing that all I could do would be to divert the Tah-tah kle-ah, maybe slow it down, throw it off. "Don't let it touch you!"

She turned then, skittering around to face the entryway, where Deace had stopped dead, an AR-15 in his hands, staring in shock at the feathered, misshapen apparition in front of him. He might have come to understand that there was something weird happening in his jurisdiction, something on a level of evil he'd never encountered before, but to be confronted with an actual monster of the Otherworld isn't something most people can take with perfect equanimity.

I shot her in the head, knocking her sideways with the shock, if not the impact. She hissed at me, a black tongue darting from behind that beak, and I advanced, keeping my crucifix up. I didn't want her to touch me, but she didn't want to get any closer to that symbol, either. "Get *out*, Deace!"

I kept driving forward, the crucifix doing more than my bullets to push the owl woman back. Strangely, though I'd had to halt the litany to yell at the sheriff, she was still shrinking away, flinching slightly.

It couldn't just be because of the crucifix. Yes, it was blessed, but it's still a symbol, an image. It doesn't have any power in and of itself.

If I hadn't been fighting for my life and Deace's, I might have sensed another presence in that place. Thinking back, I'm pretty sure my guardian angel was there, adding his own influence to any grace I could have asked for with the litany.

The Tah-tah kle-ah's reluctance to come near that crucifix was opening up some room. I could *feel* her hate, and even while those overly large, dark eyes were squinted against a glare that I couldn't see, I could tell she was looking for an opening, some way to get me to put the crucifix down so she could rip out my throat.

That wasn't happening, but that was also why having Deace inside was so dangerous.

I decided to chance it, and dashed through the opening toward Deace, hoping and praying that he didn't panic and shoot me by accident. I almost brushed the owl witch's wing as I ran, putting another bullet into her just to be on the safe side.

Maybe not so safe. I felt a pain in my side even as I shot her, suggesting that her curse was growing in strength. Protection from on high though I might have, that was generally more along the lines of protection from the more spiritual side of the fight, not actual physical harm.

I sure had the scars to prove that after all this time.

Fortunately, Deace still had enough presence of mind to recognize the difference between feathered monster and a man in jeans and a barn coat, and he lifted his muzzle as I barreled toward him, just before I slammed into him, dragging him toward the door. He wasn't ready to move, though, so instead of sweeping him to the exit and out into the sunlight, I tripped, and we both went down in a heap.

The Tah-tah kle-ah's talon went right over us as we fell, and I rolled to one side, getting off Deace—who was gasping for breath since I'd knocked the wind out of him—and swinging the crucifix back up again.

She reared back, staggering as I shot her again, feeling another blow to my chest as I did so, and she slipped on a fallen tile and crashed into the opposite wall.

Trying to ignore the ache in my chest, I scrambled to my feet, pulling Deace after me. He was a big man and not in the greatest shape, so it wasn't easy, and I was getting ever more aware of how badly this was going. I had to finish this quickly, before a bullet meant to slow her down put me far enough out of action that she could reach me.

I all but threw Deace through the door, though it was more of a shove given his weight and the fatigue that was already starting to take its toll. He staggered through the opening, and I followed, plunging out into the blinding sunlight, grabbing him by the belt and dragging him with me as I lunged out of the fatal funnel of the door, my 1911 pointed back the way we'd come.

The crucifix was probably going to be more effective at that point, but some old habits die hard.

The owl witch was still there, though she didn't want to come out into the light. She lurked in the doorway, hissing, staring at me with raw, naked hate in her eyes.

"What *is* that?" Deace gasped.

Rather than answer, I steered him toward the gate, which he'd fortunately opened. I needed to move fast.

Letting go as soon as I was sure that he was moving, I sprinted to my truck, yanking the door open and fishing around in the back for the coach gun.

It wasn't anything fancy, just an old, beat up Stoeger double barrel twelve-gauge. I cracked the action open, more by instinct and habit than necessity, and verified that it was loaded. I didn't check that I had the exorcised rock salt rounds loaded. That was a given; they were about all I had in terms of shotgun shells.

Turning back toward the sanitarium, stuffing half a dozen more shells into a coat pocket, I stalked past Sheriff Deace, who was leaning on his knees, panting, probably more from the adrenaline than the actual exertion of the brief time he'd been in the fight. "You're not going back in there."

"I'm not leaving that thing to have its way after dark." I suspected that it had entered the sanitarium the night before, while I'd been confronting the apparition on the riverbank. This had been a setup.

Deace straightened, though I barely noticed, already being well past him, halfway to the door. "I can't let you go in there alone." That brought me up short, and I turned to face him as he picked up his rifle and started to follow.

"Stay here, Sheriff." I would have tried to be a little diplomatic, but my voice was a harsh rasp, my throat raw. "I've got this, and I don't need you putting yourself at risk with this thing. You can't hurt it. I can."

For a second, I thought he was going to argue. I could see it written on his face. This was his jurisdiction. He was the law. I was a drifter with a truck full of guns and a silver crucifix around his neck.

But he'd trusted me for a reason, and while I might not appear to be entirely in control of the situation, I wasn't running in panic, either. I looked him in the eye and tried to *will* him to believe me, though I knew full well that wasn't going to happen.

Working on the spiritual side of the war more often than not, you start to understand what's doable, and what's a slip-n-slide to damnation, and mind control is definitely on the latter end of the spectrum. I wasn't trying to cast a spell on him or use telepathy or anything. I was just praying that he'd let me do my job without having to worry about the Tah-tah kle-ah ripping his head off.

Finally, he nodded, and I turned back toward the doorway without another word.

Words take time. Time we didn't have.

Chapter 8

As soon as I saw that the creature had disappeared from the doorway, I shook my head and grimaced. It had retreated back into the darkness of the old sanitarium, and I was now back to square one. If I'd moved faster, maybe I could have caught her in the entryway, shot her through the heart or the head—I still didn't know which one was going to work—and been done with this.

I shook my head again as I carefully pied off the door before making entry. I was kidding myself if I really believed that. There was no way this thing was going to make it easy. She might be more vicious and less clever than I'd expected, but she still wasn't going to stand around and wait for me to finish her off.

If I hadn't had a responsibility, I would have left her in there and thanked Heaven for getting out alive. But Witch Hunters don't have that luxury.

My boots crunched in the debris in the entryway as I carefully worked my way inside, careful to sweep all angles with the shotgun. Passing from light to dark to light and back to dark again made it hard to see, and I didn't exactly have a weapon light on a Stoeger side by side, a weapon that wouldn't have been out of place on a stagecoach seat in 1870. But I'd had practice, and I moved out of the doorway, keeping my back to the wall as I kept the shotgun up and let my eyes adjust.

With some monsters I'd hunted, that would still be a bad idea. They can get through the cracks in the wall, suddenly appearing where no human being ever could. Most of those were the ones closest to the Abyss, things that had gone farther down the road of evil until they got abilities that were truly unnatural.

Very little of the Otherworld is *naturally* the way that it is. These things aren't animals with genus and species. Even when there are similarities, like the Tah-tah kle-ah and La Lechuza, every creature stalking the world just out of sight is dangerously unique.

That's why there's no encyclopedia of the Otherworld we can consult. The patterns might all be similar, but they rarely manifest exactly the same.

My eyes got used to the dimness. It wasn't *dark*, really. The broken windows and half-collapsed roof on the south wing let in quite a bit of sunlight, but it was dim enough compared to outside that I needed the time.

There was no sign of the owl witch. She had retreated somewhere out of sight—and probably somewhere I was unlikely to suspect. With a sigh, I started to move deeper in.

I stopped after a few steps, my eyes narrowing as I scanned the mottled light and shadow in the hallway. Something told me to hold where I was.

Part of it, I was sure, was mainly that I didn't want to go room to room, hunting something that was guaranteed to try to ambush me.

"Well?" My voice echoed in the tiled hallway, startlingly loud in the quiet that had descended since I'd stopped shooting. Of course, my hearing was deadened already from the gunfire I'd unleashed in there, and it would take a little while for my ears to recover—at least somewhat. The tinnitus and hearing loss was pretty cumulative since the

Marine Corps. "You said I was going to die soon. I'm still breathing." I forced a laugh, though it was more of a bark. "Your masters in the Abyss letting you down? They tend to do that, you know."

I was swinging in the dark, but there was a good chance that something would hit home. The evil things in the Otherworld—and there are certainly neutral to benign Otherworlders, the reasons for which I've never *quite* figured out—are all beholden to the Abyss, to some degree or another. Like with humans—and a lot of Otherworlders had been human once—the Abyss doesn't actually care about the deals they make. The more power they give, the more likely they're going to screw over their client, just to get their soul.

Imagine something as old as the universe itself, that came into existence with all its knowledge. And all that knowledge could fill the collective libraries of the world several times over, before even delving into the stuff that we mere mortals have no idea about.

Now imagine that that creature can affect the world with an act of sheer will. Just a thought. It doesn't need to lift a finger, because, when all is said and done, it doesn't *have* fingers. It just needs to think and it's there.

And it hates you. You, personally. Not so much that it wants your mortal life to end—though it does—but it wants you to suffer for all of eternity, just for being human.

That's the sort of thing that exists in the Abyss. And it gives people and Otherworldly creatures power solely to corrupt them and drag them down into the darkness and the fire with it.

For a long moment, only silence greeted my taunt. It wasn't rising to the bait.

Maybe it knew what I had in that shotgun. The Tah-tah kle-ah wasn't just a monster, but a witch, as well. Its English might have been broken, but that was more because of that beak than any sort of lack of understanding.

"Nothing?" I got louder. "Cat got your tongue? Maybe those bullets hurt worse than you wanted me to think. Maybe all those stories about owl witch curses and being unkillable are just so much bullcrap." I laughed again.

That got to it.

One thing I learned a long time ago was that the creatures of the Otherworld are, above all, afflicted with overweening pride in their power. They are the things that go bump in the night, capable of things that ordinary mortal men can't do, and whatever they've sacrificed to give them that power, they still think it makes them superior.

A screech echoed through the whole building, far louder than my taunts, loud enough that the sound alone put a spike of pain through my ears, never mind the sorcerous impact of its sheer malice.

She hadn't retreated just to nurse her wounds and make it harder for me to find her with a shotgun blast. She'd been working something.

The shadows in the hallway seemed to deepen, and a wisp of what looked like smoke crawled its way along the ceiling. That metallic burned blood smell intensified, and my head really started to hurt.

"Here we go." There was more weariness and resignation in my voice than anything else. Taking a deep breath, redolent of the unnatural stink of sorcery, I started the litany from the top, beginning with the invocation and rolling right into it, still keeping the shotgun at high ready, watching and waiting for the owl woman to show herself.

The rustle and scratch of her movements weren't easily located, and not just because of the weird acoustics in the old, abandoned building. They seemed to shift from one end to the other, as if she was in one place, then in another, all without visibly moving.

It was a trick, that much I was pretty sure of, but it was a trick that could still get me killed if I was looking toward the noise while she appeared in the opposite direction. So, I kept scanning, careful not to get too invested in following the sounds.

A crash echoed through the building from the south wing, as another part of the already sagging ceiling fell in. Involuntarily, I turned toward it, the twin muzzles of my Stoeger shifting to find the target, and that gave her her opening.

Another splintering crash and clatter sounded, much closer than the collapse down the south wing. Debris smashed onto the floor as the ceiling broke through, filled with black, oily smoke and a feathered, inhuman shape as she dropped to the floor, spreading her wings as she cleared the hole.

She was already using those wings to throw herself straight at me by the time I realized what was happening. For a second, all I saw out of the corner of my eye was a black shape, wreathed in twisting shadows, throwing itself toward me, the eyes, once black, now a lurid, glowing red.

I'd like to say that I dodged quickly and smoothly, but the truth is that I flinched. I started so hard that I just about fell over, and that was the only thing that saved me. Jerking myself backward, my silver crucifix swung on its chain, exposing the owl witch to it.

Despite the fact she was all hopped up on sorcery and dark power, she still *really* didn't care for that emblem of

His sacrificial charity. She twisted, almost managing to halt herself in midair, throwing herself halfway across the hallway to get away from that crucifix. She'd been hoping to blindside me, kill me from behind where she wouldn't have to look at it.

That nearly impossible dodge gave me *my* opening. Recovering from my fright, I swung the shotgun up and fired.

Now, I was rattled. That's my excuse for doubling the Stoeger, anyway.

Most people think that when you fire both barrels at once in a double-barreled twelve gauge, it doubles the recoil. That's not how ballistics works, though. It doesn't double the recoil.

It *quadruples* it.

I was already off balance, and I wasn't holding the shotgun in what I'd call a solid shooting position, so when both barrels went off, that side by side kicked me so hard I just about lost my grip on it. I almost didn't even see what the first blast had done, while I desperately scrambled to reload, snapping the action open and sending the spent casings flying while I dug into my pocket for another pair.

Only as I snapped the shotgun closed again did I look up and see what the first shot had done. I'd been moving, too, and I was already across the entryway and almost halfway down the north hall before I was ready to shoot again. I didn't want to give her a stationary target, at the same time there was no way I was going to turn my back on her again.

She was actually in worse shape than I'd feared. Now, rock salt tends to explode when there's enough force exerted on it, and I suspect that half of those two shots had been turned to table salt as soon as the gun had gone off.

Don't get me wrong, at the right range it'll hurt, but it's not like buckshot or anything.

If you're talking about a normal, mortal man or animal.

The witch was staggering, smoke pouring from half a dozen holes in her chest. Feathers were curling and withering where the salt had struck her.

The *exorcised* salt.

I held my fire as I advanced, much of my equilibrium regained, though my heart was still trying to jackhammer its way out of my chest. I leveled the coach gun at her head as I got closer, and this time I only pulled one trigger.

Boom. My hearing was going to be like being underwater for the next week. I almost flinched at the concussion of my own weapon, but I kept it leveled, looking over the twin barrels as the salt smashed into the Tah-tah kle-ah's head.

The side of the owl-witch's skull was smashed in, more smoke rising from the impact point. It was almost like the skull beneath the feathers was as thin as an actual bird's. I knew it wasn't, but the unnatural and sorcerous can't stand up to the holy. Not for long.

With a last, despairing cry, that didn't even seem to come from the monster's lungs, she slumped to the floor.

I kept the shotgun trained on the crumpled, still, smoking form, and finished the litany that I'd barely registered that I'd started. Then I crossed myself, tucked the shotgun under my arm, and reached down to seize the owl woman by the leg. She was surprisingly light. The flesh beneath the feathers was already visibly withering.

I dragged the body out into the sunlight. It didn't smoke any more. As far as I knew, the Tah-tah kle-ah isn't vulnerable to sunlight the way, say, vampires are.

They just prefer the dark, because their works are evil.

I looked up at Deace, who was staring at the corpse I was dragging, his eyes wide. "Is there an incinerator around here?" I asked. "I think we probably ought to burn it, just in case."

Chapter 9

Deace didn't say much as we loaded the increasingly dry, brittle corpse of the owl witch into my truck. Finally, still staring at the feathered monstrosity, he said, "There's a crematorium in the county morgue. I don't know of any other incinerator that might take that… whatever it is."

I shook my head. "As much as I'm not really a fan of cremation, the fact is that a crematorium has been used for the interment of regular people. In a way, it's still sacred." I looked down at the owl witch's remains with a grimace. Who knew just how old that thing was? "Disposing of this in it would be something of a desecration."

Deace shrugged, clearly still plenty uncomfortable. "I don't know what else to do. There's no incinerator in the county big enough for that."

I grimaced. I wasn't going to give this thing the dignity of a burial. There were a number of reasons for that, not least that whatever had made the owl witch had opened a door, and there was a possibility—however remote—that if I left the body intact, something else might crawl into it.

"Well, I guess we're going to have to do this the old-fashioned way, then." I looked over at Deace. "You know anywhere we can make a bonfire? A big one?"

Something seemed to click behind his eyes, though he was still focused on the monster, still rattled by the reality of what had been in his county. "Yeah, I know a place." He didn't move toward his own vehicle yet, though. His eyes were still riveted on the Tah-tah kle-ah. He looked like a man searching for words.

"Is that… Is that the thing that's been killing people? Really?"

I shook my head again, and I saw his face fall. He'd been hoping that this was over, that I'd solved his problem. "No. It hadn't been in there very long, in fact I suspect that it only flew in last night. There'd be more signs if it had a nest in that building." I glanced over my shoulder at the sanitarium. "It seems like a logical place for something haunting this area to hole up, but that just made it a good place to set a trap." I sighed, my eyes turning to the bluffs above the town. "No, this thing was sent to get me off the track. Kill me, if possible, drive me away if not. For one thing, while I'm no expert on them, I'm pretty sure that a Tah-tah kle-ah can't be killed by hanging, can't appear to be an ordinary human being anymore, and can't come back once it *is* dead." My lip curled. "This is more complicated than I was afraid it was going to be."

"What do we do, then?" He was watching me, no longer with the look of a man who was trying to judge whether or not to lock me up, but with the look of a man who was very much hoping I had an answer.

"First things first. We burn this thing." I started toward my cab. "Show me where we can build a pyre."

***

The flames crackled as they licked at the withering feathers. The impression that the owl witch's body had turned dry and brittle as soon as the exorcised salt had finally killed it hadn't been that far off. We'd splashed it with diesel after we'd laid it on the pile of pallets and old, busted up barn wood, but the way it was burning it might not have needed it. The carcass would be ashes in short order.

"So, if that wasn't the thing we're after…" Deace was staring at the flames. He was handling this better than some I'd worked with, but he was still trying to wrap his head around the weirdness. It's one thing to deal with a serial killer that appeared to be somehow related to a string of occult killings going back over a hundred years. He might have thought that I could help with my crucifix, holy water, and old guns, but I doubted that, deep down, he'd really thought there were actual monsters involved. Maybe some occult stuff that I might know more about, or something.

There's a part of the human mind that can partially accept that there's some weird stuff going on without fully grasping what that means. Some of that is a defense mechanism, a bias toward normalcy. The creatures of the Otherworld can be twisted manifestations of madness, and if the demons of the Abyss can break a man's mind, they will. It's not that hard for them; they operate on a different level of existence, one that we weren't designed for, not in this life.

Deace was being forced to confront the fact that he couldn't just accept the weird in the abstract anymore. It was concrete now, and if something like the owl witch was real, what else was?

"Now what do we do?" I finished his question. I sighed. "To start with, I'd suggest that people stay inside and lock their doors after dark. Everyone in town. Whatever this thing is, it's not going to let this go unanswered. It sent a Tat-tah kle-ah after me, and I killed it. It's going to be angry."

He eyed me. "Maybe I should stay with you."

I shook my head. I'd certainly been in spots where I would have appreciated backup, and there had been a few outsiders who'd stepped up and performed well in that role. Mostly cops and vets, if I were being honest. But when I didn't even know exactly what I was up against, I didn't want Deace getting in the way.

And I wasn't worried that he'd get in *my* way, either. Let the monster that was tearing people up and depositing its trophies around the town find him between it and me, and he was meat.

Especially if, like the owl witch, it wasn't something that could be killed with regular bullets, and the stories about its "executions" seemed to gravitate that way.

Assuming it's just one and not a nest.

Boy, Jed, you really are quite the optimist, aren't you?

"I need you to keep a lid on the town and the nearby area while I do some more looking around. The obvious spot turned out to be an ambush, which means this thing is a bit more subtle than I expected." I sighed. "This could take some time. The less people are out and exposed where this thing can get to them, the better."

"I can't just shut the county down."

"I know." It was tough, and while I dreaded to think about it, I knew that some more people were going to die before this was over. Unless I got a sign from on high pretty soon, pointing out my quarry, this was going to take time, time during which the adversary was going to be able to retaliate.

It might just hunt me, but something told me that it would lash out at the locals first. I couldn't put my finger on why I knew that, but it was there, nonetheless.

"Do what you can. But these people are going to need you, and I can't afford to lose you to this thing if it decides to come after me." I thought it over.

The thought hit me rather suddenly. "What do you know about a guy named Harper? Said he's fairly new in town, has an interest in these killings?"

He frowned. "Harper Riddle? He's a rich Silicon Valley type who bought the old Dermody house a while back. Nobody's gotten very close to him. He's kinda weird, if I'm being honest."

I had to laugh. "As opposed to a drifter passing through with a silver crucifix and a truck full of guns and holy water?"

Deace shrugged. "His kind of weird hasn't killed a monster in the old asylum." He shook his head. "Actually, it goes a little deeper than just being a little off. He's some Silicon Valley type. Rich enough that he doesn't need to work, so he just hangs around, asks questions, takes pictures, and…other things."

"What other things?"

"He's never been caught, but there have been weird graffiti scrawled in places where he's been seen loitering. Most of it looks like some sort of pictographs or something. Freaky, though. They tend to make people feel weird looking at them. Sean told me he actually felt a little sick after he'd been around one for a while."

My eyes narrowed. "Glyphs." They were sorcerous symbols, designed to invoke powers of varying potencies. Some were summons for Otherworlders, some were invocations of demons.

Deace seemed a little flustered, but he drove on. "We've cleaned them up where we've found them. Again, he's never been caught, but I was watching him once as he passed a spot where one of them had been found. He seemed a little upset that it wasn't there anymore."

"That's a bit of a warning sign, all right." I shook my head. I'd called it. Harper Riddle was playing with fire, at best. The question was, how was he actually connected with the killer around here? "Anything else?"

"I've had to chase him away from crime scenes a few times."

With a glance at him, I studied Deace's manner. There was something about the way he'd said that...

"I take it these were the crime scenes left by our predator?"

He gulped and nodded. He was probably remembering some pretty gruesome stuff, and he didn't care for the recollection.

"Did he try to take anything?" From the way that Deace's face stiffened a little, I already knew the answer before he said anything.

"Yes, he did. I caught him a couple of times, but I suspect that he took something the other times, and I just didn't know it." He took a deep breath, clearly even more uncomfortable. "I took what he'd taken; it was evidence. It was pretty gruesome stuff, too. I don't know if he was just some sick collector, or if there's something else going on.

I glanced at the fire, which was finally starting to die down, the owl-witch having turned mostly to ash. Most bodies didn't burn that fast, but the unnatural warping that had not only changed the woman's form, but presumably kept her alive far beyond the regular human lifespan, had its drawbacks.

A Tah-tah kle-ah was big, bad medicine. That it had apparently been acting as a minion for something else was not comforting.

"I'm going to have to go talk to him." I watched the last of the monstrous corpse crumble to ash in the flames.

"There's something else going on there, and while I should say that I *don't* think he's directly connected with our predator, he's into something he probably shouldn't be. That might be making things worse."

Deace had turned to study me as soon as I'd said that about something being off about the man. That was why I had to add the caveat that I didn't think Riddle was the source of the trouble. Something about the way he'd reacted during our brief conversation at the cemetery bothered me, though.

I turned toward my truck. "Keep your eyes open, Sheriff. I'll be in touch."

Chapter 10

Unfortunately, things were moving faster than I was. I didn't get far before all hell broke loose.

It had been a pretty nice day, despite the encounter with the owl-witch. A few fluffy clouds had been hovering near the horizon, but that was about it. The forecast on the radio had been for more of the same.

So, when I was half a mile from the farm where Deace and I had burned the Tah-tah kle-ah, and the black clouds started to boil up out of nowhere, I knew that we were in for it.

The sunny afternoon quickly turned into twilight, split by a bolt of downright purple lightning. I grimaced as I looked up at the lowering sky.

"Oh, boy." I shook my head and kept driving as the rain and hail started, the thunderclap rolling overhead like the universe's biggest drum. "Well, at least it ain't blood or frogs this time."

The storm quickly got worse as I rolled toward where Deace had said Harper Riddle's house was. Visibility dropped to a few hundred feet in moments, as the clouds blotted out the sky and the rain and hail got thicker and came down harder. Some of the impacts made me worry that my windshield was about to crack under the hammering.

More of that violet lightning split the sky. This was definitely no natural storm.

Finally, I had to stop. I simply couldn't see, and the wind and rain were rocking my truck, which took some doing. To make my assessment even grimmer, as soon as I backed up, the pressure seemed to ease, though the darkness remained.

Yeah. Someone or something didn't want anyone leaving the town. This was bad.

I found a place to turn around. It stuck in my craw, knowing that I was, in a way, backing down in front of the forces of evil, but there are some things—a lot of things, actually—that we don't have any control over. Whatever was going on, I wasn't supposed to confront Harper just yet.

That may sound fatalistic, but the fact of the matter is that the Otherworld and the Abyss don't actually get to do much of anything without it being allowed. That infuriates the demons and the monsters to no end, and it bends some human minds who can't get the fact that this is being allowed to happen for our benefit.

It just doesn't usually feel that way.

I sat in my truck for a moment, buffeted by the weather, including the thunderclap from yet another lightning bolt that tracked across the clouds directly over the road. In fact, it was weirdly straight, almost as if it were following the road.

Well, if this was the sorcerous weather that I suspected it was, then all sorts of unnatural, weird stuff was to be expected.

Finally, biting back a curse that would have fit more when I'd been a Marine, before I'd taken the cross as a Witch Hunter, I turned around and headed back to town. This storm wasn't a coincidence, not coming so quickly on the heels of my killing of the owl-witch. This was intended to blot out the day so that the predator could walk.

There was something in the dark, and it had just brought the dark to it.

As I drove back into town, it actually seemed to get darker, which I wouldn't have thought was quite possible. It was like the epicenter of the storm was directly over Leutenburg. If I'd had any doubt that this was a preternatural phenomenon—and I didn't—that would have dispelled it.

I was nearing the outskirts of town, getting down into the low ground, the road lined with trees which were lashing in the wind, the shadows beneath them almost pitch black through the dimness and the rain. The first lights were becoming visible through the curtains of water and ice sluicing off my windshield as I got closer to the car lot and the old grain elevator on the outskirts of town.

I stomped on the brake as movement flickered ahead of me. I squinted through the driving rain but while *something* ran across the road, it was too dark to see what.

As soon as I started moving again, it happened again. This time I got a little bit better glimpse, but still not enough to identify anything except that it had four limbs and was running or bounding on all four of them.

It also seemed to be pitch black and completely featureless. Almost like a shadow had just run across the road.

That wasn't good. Not that anything about this situation was.

While it is true that even these horrifying situations are allowed to happen for a reason, that doesn't mean we can't still go down the hard way. The one truth in this life is that you don't get out of it alive, though how you meet that end is far more important than most people think.

I stopped the truck, watching the street in front of me. I could tell now that not all the lights ahead were just porch lights and signs. Blue flashers were blinking somewhere down the street, distorted in the driving rain. If I listened carefully, I could have sworn that I heard gunshots.

With a deep breath, I dragged my Winchester to me, shouldered into my old Gore-Tex, and got out.

I didn't want to lose this truck the way I'd lost my old F-100. There was no sign of any giant, tar-like toad demon around yet, but with this storm going on, I wasn't going to take any chances. Besides, fighting monsters from inside a truck rarely works out well.

And from the sight of those shadowy shapes running across the road, there were monsters in the storm that needed to be fought.

The predator hadn't come alone.

I should have expected that after the asylum, but I was starting to get pissed. This thing was toying with me now, and it was making me angry.

It was still possible that it really considered me a threat—or, more accurately, the authority by which I hunted things like it—but somehow it still felt different. This thing was over a century old—if not much, much older—and it had willingly and laughingly gone to the gallows multiple times. I doubted that it was truly afraid of little old me with my guns, silver, iron, and holy water.

It should be, but I'd been around these sorts of things before. "Titanically arrogant" was probably the best description.

Slamming the door shut, I hunched my shoulders against the storm as it lashed at me. Even with the Gore-Tex, I was soaked in seconds. The storm was driving the rain and hail right into my face. If one of those little shadow creatures had tried to jump me right then, it probably would have won.

But I was alone on the road, facing the lights of the grain elevator, peering toward the flashing blue light bar of a sheriff's department vehicle a quarter mile or so ahead. If I was remembering things right, that was probably right in front of the diner where Sheriff Deace had first "arrested" me.

That probably wasn't a good sign, either, given the time of day.

The temptation to just charge in and help, as I heard more gunshots and a high, thin screeching, was intense, but I resisted it. The Good Lord looks out for fools and small children, but He doesn't expect His warriors to be fools. I needed to move carefully to make sure I wasn't about to get eviscerated by something with too many teeth and claws before I even got close to the diner.

I circled around the back of my truck first, my Winchester in my hands. The old, blued steel and walnut rifle was going to need some serious work after being out in this storm, but it was hardly the first time.

Nothing jumped out at me at first. I was sure I saw a pair of red eyes peering at me from behind one of the grain elevators, but they vanished as soon as I swept them with my rifle's muzzle. Even if those eyes belonged something bulletproof, four hundred five grains of lead and silver was gonna hurt.

I faded toward the car lot. There were a lot of places for the monsters to hide in there, but I'd seen the eyes by the grain elevator, and that was also where those dark forms had raced to when they'd crossed the road in front of me. It was possible that they were just phantoms, illusions conjured up to try to get me to wreck, but I had to be careful.

It took time to work my way along the side of the road, pieing off each angle as I passed it. There are tactics that don't translate well between mortal warfare and monster hunting, but again, sometimes old habits die hard, and it wasn't as if I were hurting by checking each angle. An Otherworldly monstrosity might be able to shrink out of sight in an extremely small space, only to pop out as soon as I turned away, but there's only so much you can do, and if I managed to get a little bit of advance warning, it might mean the difference between surviving the storm and getting ripped to shreds.

This job is often an odd juxtaposition of regular combat tactics and supernatural, spiritual struggle.

I got past the car lot and the grain elevator without having to fend off some twisted mass of teeth and claws. In fact, I hadn't seen any of the little shadowy things again, making me wonder all over again if they hadn't just been illusions intended to throw me off. Or maybe they were just manifestations of some of the things drawn by the sorcery that had summoned the storm.

Things like this drew lesser spirits and monsters like flies to a corpse.

The noise from the diner was getting louder, clearer through the roar and thunder of the storm. The gunshots were getting more sporadic, while the screeching and howling got louder. I picked up the pace, even as I did my utmost to avoid turning my back on any openings.

I was getting close enough that I could see some of the chaos inside the diner. It was still just violent movement, things flying around, but I thought I could see, through one broken window, something leaping up and down on top of one of the tables.

It didn't look very large. It didn't look human, either.

I faded toward the corner, trying to get a better view of what I was about to charge into. Just because all hell was breaking loose wasn't a good reason to get ahead of myself. Getting my throat ripped out wouldn't help anyone inside.

The diner was a disaster area. Tables and chairs had been flipped over and smashed. The staff and clientele—a good number of people, since it was the lunch hour—were behind the counter with the sheriff's deputy who had left his vehicle out front. They were hunkered down as the creatures around them hopped and screeched and threw things. So far, the monsters hadn't tried to storm the counter, but the broken, battered shape dragging itself away from the counter, even as its limbs seemed to creak back into place as it crawled, told me that they were still putting up a fight. At least one figure behind that counter had a skillet in hand.

The creatures were small, none taller than about three feet. They were humanoid, but they definitely weren't human. Pot-bellied, winged mockeries of man, they had mouths full of shark teeth and stubby bat wings. Their limbs were about as stubby as the wings, with gnarled, clawed hands that clutched clubs, stone axes, and spears. From where I stood, I could see at least a couple of them only had one eye. One was an actual cyclops, with a large, glaring orb right in the center of its forehead. The other had a twisted mass of scar tissue where its right eye might have been before.

There were any number of savage little people in American Indian legend. Which ones these were didn't matter that much—remember what I said about trying to classify the Otherworld—except for what it was going to take to kill them.

Even as I moved closer, the deputy popped over the counter with his pistol and shot another of the creatures as it jumped off a nearby table toward the besieged townspeople. He was better with the gun than a lot of cops I'd seen, and he double tapped it neatly center mass. The impacts staggered it, and it landed badly, the diner and the waitress closest to it battering at it with kitchen utensils.

I was a little surprised that the clientele weren't packing, but then it turned out that I was wrong. Another of the locals, a woman in her late thirties or forties, came up over the counter with a Glock in her fist and shot another of the little creatures as it hopped up onto another nearby table.

The bullets hit and staggered the tiny monstrosities, but they didn't seem to do any serious damage. That wasn't good.

The time for observation and orientation was past. It was time to decide and act.

I briefly considered just going through the broken window in front of me, but I dismissed that idea pretty quickly. I was going to get caught on broken glass, provided I didn't get shot by one of the nearly panicked people behind the counter.

So, I leveled my Winchester, hoped that either the silver or iron was going to do the trick, and shot the nearest pot-bellied dwarf center mass, putting my gold bead right below the root of its wing.

I'd actually almost forgotten which I had loaded first, the iron rounds or the silver. Lead and copper clearly wasn't doing much, which meant that—like the owl-witch—these things were going to require something a little bit more on the symbolic side. Some Otherworlders are susceptible to silver, though there are differing opinions as to why. Others go down to iron, the prevailing theory being that there is a connection to the nails on the Cross.

As it turned out, I had an iron shot first, a 40-grain iron ball set into the .45 caliber bullet's hollow point. The .45-70 was effectively a flying sledgehammer already, and the iron set in the nose of the bullet punched right through the creature's tough hide. It folded like a cheap suit and collapsed with a yawp that still made my ears hurt even over the gunfire.

The others didn't take long to react. They scattered to the corners of the diner like startled quail, screeching and howling. They weren't entirely panicked, though, as several of those stone-tipped spears came streaking my way, two of them sailing out into the night through the broken window, three more hammering into the brick wall of the diner, punching deep enough into the bricks that I knew that I really *did not* want to get hit by one of those.

Seems intuitive enough, of course. Don't get stuck by the pointy thing thrown by a shark-toothed little monster. But it went beyond the risk of getting a new hole poked in me.

Whatever these things were, I could probably be pretty sure those spears—and the rest of their weapons—were probably cursed. That wasn't necessarily as immediately fatal as poison might be, but it wasn't anything that anyone sane wanted to take chances with, silver crucifix or no.

I had ducked behind the column of brick that formed the corner of the building, though its cover wasn't nearly as substantial as I might have hoped. As those spears thudded into the wall—hard enough that I could feel it with my back to the brick, which wasn't good, either—I shoved a fresh round into the loading gate and then pivoted back, dropping my Winchester's muzzle and searching for another target.

Another cyclops with its single, baleful eye filling its entire forehead was streaking toward me, its mouth agape, a stone tomahawk in one clawed fist. I shot it on the wing, though the silver didn't do much. Like the regular copper and lead bullets the locals had been using, it knocked it back, but that was about it as I racked another round into the chamber, the spent casing spinning off into the dark and the wet over my shoulder.

The creature tumbled through the air before arresting its movement and coming back at me again. There was no way those wings were actually keeping any of them aloft; that was sorcery, plain and simple.

Not that I needed any more reason to put these things down.

My second shot took it in the mouth. The iron did its job, blasting dark gore out of the back of the thing's misshapen skull, and it dropped like a rock, crashing onto a table and rolling off as it cracked the tabletop.

They were heavier than they looked.

The next shot knocked another one sprawling, but while the bullet half caved in its head, it didn't penetrate, and the skull started to reform as soon as it popped back up from the booth I'd blasted it into. I hated wasting the silver rounds. They weren't cheap. But it wasn't as if I could unload the rifle and just put iron rounds in.

As the thing clambered over the back of the bench, the sheriff's deputy shot it again, the 9mm rounds knocking the creature around but without doing much more than getting its attention. It pivoted and screamed at him, at which point I blew the top of its skull off. It fell out of sight.

Then I had my hands full, as another pair of the things came around behind me, whooping and clawing at each other to get to me. I ducked and threw myself into the street, swinging my rifle to catch one of them with the barrel like a baseball bat. The impact was jarring, though hitting the soaked pavement a moment later was worse as I almost got the wind knocked out of me. The creature flew backward a couple of feet, but it wasn't nearly the home run that I might have hoped for. The second dove at me, and I barely got a boot up and kicked it.

It was like kicking a rock, and the shock actually pushed me a couple inches backward, but it knocked the creature back just far enough that I was able to swing my rifle to bear again, and when it recovered and started to dart toward me again, it came up against the muzzle and I blasted it.

Of course, that was another of the silver rounds, not an iron, so I just bought myself a few inches of space again, but that was enough to work the lever and blast it with another iron round.

I realized that I'd lost track of how many rounds I'd fired. That could get bad, but I still had at least one more of those things coming at me, the dent I'd put in its skull with my rifle barrel already reforming as it flattened its wings back and came right at my face, stone knife in one hand, its jaws agape.

Rolling to my side, I blasted it twice, as fast as I could work the lever, the first round knocking it back, the second punching a fist sized hole out through its back.

Then I knew I was empty, and I didn't have time to take cover and reload. I drew my 1911 and got ready to go to work as I levered myself up off the street.

A part of me, a part that had still remained somewhat detached and analytical through the fight, noticed that the swarm of the little creatures that I'd expected to dogpile me as soon as I'd gone down in the street hadn't materialized. I hadn't exactly had a chance to count the vicious little terrors, but I was sure there were still more of them in there.

More gunfire barked inside, but I already knew it wasn't going to do much except put me at risk. "Hold your fire!" I was still down on the sidewalk, but a bullet had just punched through the remains of one of the windows, entirely too close to my head.

Three more shots sounded from inside before they stopped shooting, and when I could hear again over the rain and the insane gibbering of the little monsters, I could hear the deputy shouting. Some of the locals were too rattled to listen to reason, it seemed.

I managed to get myself behind the brick column again, double checking the mag in my 1911. I had, indeed, grabbed an iron mag. Good. "I'm coming in! Watch your fire!" The little pot-bellied horrors were still in there, but something had changed, and I needed to find out what without getting my head blown off.

The deputy was yelling, and it took a second through all the other noise to realize that *he* was the one who was still trying to fight, and some of the other locals were restraining him. This was awkward, but I peered around the brick corner with my pistol leveled, in time to see what I really hadn't wanted to see.

One of the more shriveled-looking creatures was on a table, hopping in a ritualized sort of pattern, chanting words that felt like ice picks in my ears. The other surviving creatures had joined it, hopping up and down in a circle around it, cracking the tabletop with each landing.

That was a shamanic invocation if ever I'd seen one, and while some people might argue that human shamans are relatively harmless—they're not—anything an Otherworld shaman does is going to come right out of the Abyss.

So, I leveled my .45 and shot the shaman in the head.

At least, I tried to.

The bullet didn't stop dead in midair, which would have been pretty nuts even in my experience. But it was definitely deflected, smacking brick dust off the far wall.

I almost expected the hopping goblins—or whatever they were—to swarm me then, but they kept at it, though at least one flipped around as it kept hopping, still chanting that grating song, and hurled its tomahawk at me. I ducked the stone weapon and shot it through the teeth, dropping it like a rock.

The others didn't even seem to notice except to close the ring a little tighter and keep hopping.

The deputy had calmed down, though the waitress who had first confronted me when I'd rolled into town was now trying to usher people out into the kitchen. I wasn't sure how good an idea that was, given the storm outside, but at least it got them out of my line of fire.

I finally moved into the diner, ducking a couple more missiles from the hopping monsters as I moved to the door, pieing off the window as I went, though I held my fire because those people were still inside, behind the counter, and I couldn't be sure exactly where.

Glass crunched under my boots as I stepped inside. The interior of the diner was getting cold, but sweat was pouring out of me as soon as I crossed the threshold. The smell of burned blood and worse was starting to grow, intensifying as I stepped closer to that table where the shaman was weaving his spell.

The rest of the savage little monsters had turned to face me, and I was ducking and weaving to avoid the flying stone weapons as they chucked them at me. They were trying desperately to keep me away from the shaman. Unfortunately for them, they were now stuck close to it. Not one of them had tried to come at me once the shaman had started its chant.

I shot one through the eyeball, another through the teeth, and a third in its protruding belly. I hadn't been *trying* to gut shoot it, not even the inhuman monstrosity that it was, but I was shooting and moving fast.

Unfortunately, it didn't seem like whittling down its bodyguard was putting any sort of a wrench in the shaman's ritual. The roar of the storm seemed to be getting louder, blending with the screeching chant, the stink was getting worse, the room was getting colder, and my head was starting to hurt as a deep fatigue started to set into my limbs.

Something was coming, and it was going to be really bad when it got there. Maybe even worse than the predator I was already hunting.

I shot two more of the hopping gremlins, or whatever they were. They dropped like rocks, and in a brief moment of clarity, I saw one of them hit the ground and start to crumble, as if it were made of clay or sand.

They weren't the biggest threat, but I had to get them out of the way. The chill deepened, and my limbs felt heavy as I shot one more, the slide locking back on an empty magazine. I quickly reloaded, but then I shoved the 1911 back into its holster as I drew my knife and closed in.

The knife by itself wasn't going to be enough, and I knew it. I began another prayer as I held the knife with one hand and drew out my holy water flask with the other.

There was a reason for the different prayer. This was one against sorcery specifically. In this kind of combat, specificity matters. That might bother some people, but the fact of the matter is that we have free will, which means no shortcuts. And where forces like this have been allowed to cut loose, there are going to be even fewer shortcuts. That would defeat the purpose.

As I kept up the prayer, unscrewing the flask's cap, the chant seemed to stutter, and the chill might have lessened slightly. The shaman looked at me with its one, swollen eye, and I shuddered involuntarily at the bleary hatred in that gaze.

Its arm twitched, and I swayed out of the way just in time, the stone knife it had just hurled going past my ear to embed itself with a *bang* in the wall behind me. A part of me wanted to shoot it, even though I knew it wouldn't do any good, just to show it how little I liked that.

I was almost within arm's reach, but despite the prayers, the fatigue was getting to me. I could barely lift the holy water flask, and the knife hung at my side like it weighed a ton. Gritting my teeth, I kept up the litany as I lifted the flask and splashed the holy water on the shaman from a little over a yard away.

It screamed and fell on its butt, its skin smoking where the holy water had struck it. I felt some of the weight lift, and I was on it in a flash, my knife rising and coming down fast and hard.

The point plunged into the thing right where the neck met the shoulder. It screamed and writhed, even as its flesh started to turn to clay and dust around the knife blade. The weariness lifted suddenly, and the cold and the stench faded. I got one more horrific glare of hatred out of the shaman's single eye before that, too, crumbled to grains of sand.

As I straightened, it occurred to me that I probably could have just stabbed the thing in the head. It wasn't as if it were a living being, with blood vessels and nerves. Old habits and training again, I guess.

I took stock. The last of the little monsters was gone, now only a series of crumbled piles of ash and dirt. The deputy was leaning against the counter, and the waitress who had hit one of the goblins with a skillet was in the door to the kitchen, staring and breathing hard.

Overhead, another roll of thunder shook the building. This wasn't over yet.

Chapter 11

I looked at the deputy. He was haggard and scared, his eyes wide as he stared unseeing past me at the piles of debris that had been vicious little people only a short time before. "Deputy Pipes!" His nametag was clear enough, anyway, and I snapped my fingers at him. "Snap out of it!" I needed this guy, even if his gun wasn't going to do squat against the monsters out in the dark and the storm.

"What *were* those things?" He finally looked up at me, finding words for the horror that he'd just witnessed.

"Monsters. Now they're dead monsters." That was a bit of a simplification, since something that crumbles to dust when you hit it wasn't alive to begin with, but this wasn't the time to nitpick. Which was also why I wasn't going to waste time speculating.

Thunder rumbled again, but it sounded fainter, farther away. Or maybe it was just weaker. The howl of the wind outside seemed to have lessened, and there was a little more light beyond the shattered windows.

"Come on. Things might be calming down after I put that thing down, but we need to see if anyone else is hurt." *Or worse*, I didn't say. He didn't need those kinds of nightmares, not if I could help it.

He gulped, still staring at the monsters and the wreckage of the diner, then nodded, struggling a little to holster his handgun. "Let's go." He didn't sound eager, and I couldn't blame him.

I led the way, while the waitress, without being asked, set to making sure all the clientele were okay. That took a bit of a load off my mind, as I hated to turn my back on terrified—and in some cases, hurt—people, but priorities were priorities. There was only one of me.

I led the way outside, into the rain-drenched streets, my boots crunching in the hail that hadn't melted yet. My Winchester was lying on the sidewalk next to the wall, and I holstered my .45 and picked it up, hastily wiping off the water and shoving eight more iron-enhanced .45-70 rounds into the tube. It was a good thing I took as good care of that rifle as I did, or I'd be in trouble.

It had been through worse, though.

Deputy Pipes was keeping close to me, though I wasn't going to mention it. From the looks of him, he was young, and though he was in good shape, I'd been around enough law enforcement not to entirely trust his training level. And even if he was one of those who trained on his own constantly, this situation was so far outside his training and experience that I needed him to stay close to me and do what I told him. The fact that he appeared disposed that way already was a good sign.

The rain and hail had let up and the wind was dying, while the light improved with the thinning of the clouds, though it remained darker than normal for the time of day. The rain was being replaced by fog, though, so I still couldn't see all that far.

Something about that fog bothered me. It was cold, but it wasn't *that* cold, and I couldn't think of a time when I'd seen fog rise right after a violent thunderstorm.

The faint smell of something metallic on the lowering breeze told me all I needed to know.

"Have you got your radio?" It might be a dumb question under other circumstances, but Pipes had seen what few people ever do, even if law enforcement regularly came up against the spooky and weird more than most of the population. He was rattled, and so I had to take that into account.

"Yeah. Who do you need me to call?"

"Call your boss." I could see the faint glow of flashing red and white lights through the mist ahead, though I realized that I couldn't see any other lights. I would have expected a lot to come on automatically, even in a Podunk town like Leutenburg, It had certainly gotten dark enough.

He keyed the radio, calling Deace. At least, I assumed that alphanumeric callsign was Deace. I wasn't paying too much attention to what he sent over the radio, since I was watching the street and looking for any sign that the monsters might have stuck around.

Sure enough, I saw movement in the mists, and it didn't move like a human being. My Winchester came up, just as it vanished, and Pipes was talking. "The sheriff is up by the hospital. He wants to know where you are and what he needs to do."

"Let's go to the hospital, then." I was beginning to suspect that the storm had been far more destructive than it had initially seemed, and the monsters running around inside it even more so. I couldn't see any lights on the street ahead or behind us, and even as I checked, the lights in the diner went out. I didn't know what kind of weirdness had kept them on while I'd been fighting the shaman and his fellow goblins, but it had probably been calculated to let the clientele see the monsters in all their grotesquery, to add to the horror. Monsters can be jerks like that.

Pipes just nodded, his SIG clenched in both hands as he peered into the mists. He wasn't going to back down, but he was rattled, and I realized just how rattled when he spun halfway around and brought that 9mm up toward the sound that he thought he'd heard.

I was going to have to keep a close eye on Pipes, just to make sure he was checking his targets before he opened fire.

While I was pretty sure I could remember where the hospital was—I might be a stranger to Leutenburg, but I had made it a habit a long time back to make sure I knew where the major landmarks were if I was going to be staying in one place for even a night—but I realized that there was more at stake here than my navigational prowess. "Why don't you lead the way, Deputy Pipes?"

I not only wanted him in front of me where I could keep track of where that handgun was pointed, but I needed him focused on something besides how scared he was.

It took a second for my suggestion to sink in, and then he nodded, swallowing, and started down the street. I kept close behind him, offset just to one side so that I could shoot past him if I needed to.

I was whispering a litany as we went. Some might say that I wasn't showing a lot of faith, that I was trying to make sure that I had Heaven's attention. The truth is that we're *supposed* to pray like that, because otherwise we might start thinking that we're doing all of it.

The punch that Winchester gave me was usually only enough to keep the really nasty stuff at bay. I had to let Higher do the rest.

We made our way down the street, toward downtown. We didn't have far to go; Leutenburg wasn't a big town. Still bigger than a few of the backcountry towns where I've had to work, but not huge.

This was the kind of town where the monsters thought they could be a little more overt. In the big cities they get sneaky, and it gets *really* hard to pin them down.

Sirens wailed. Leutenburg Fire was busy, and as I saw a burgeoning reddish glow through the fog, I could imagine why. I didn't think that was only because of lightning strikes, either, especially given the amount of rain and hail that had pelted the town out of the blue.

Something skittered in the dark off to my right, and I shifted my muzzle toward it, even as Pipes jerked and spun around, looking for the monster about to leap out of the murk and eat his face off. "Easy, Deputy." I saw nothing, and I made the sign of the cross as I lifted my rifle toward the sky. "Don't get too trigger happy. Some of these things will try to scare you into shooting at shadows, and they're clever enough to do it where you're likely to hit a kid or something on the other side. Know your target and consider its background, remember?"

He took a deep breath, lowering the weapon, and nodded. "Right." He glanced at me. "They'd really do that?"

I had my Winchester back at a high ready. "They're evil, Deputy. Evil like you've never seen before. Damn straight they'd do that."

He shuddered. That was saying something. This might be a small town, but the bucolic little slice of rural Americana where nothing that bad happened was a thing of the past, more so now than it ever had been. People blamed politics, industry moving elsewhere, the weather, or any number of other things, but the truth was that the monsters and the demons had gotten more and more of a foothold, the last few decades, and even though it had always been a bad idea to think that there was any place that was immune to them, it was even less so now. They were always in the background, giving a push to the broken homes, the drugs, and the increasing violent crime.

Watching mankind destroy itself is the closest they ever come to joy.

We kept moving, staying on the sidewalk as another fire truck went by, red lights flashing, heading for the fire I'd seen through the mist. I thought I saw more shadows moving in the murk, almost as if they were following us to either side, but if the goblins or whatever they were had friends, they weren't eager to tangle with us.

The silver crucifix hanging from its leather thong around my neck might have had something to do with that, even more than the threat of my big-bore Winchester.

More flashing lights pointed the way, and we found ourselves in front of the hospital kind of suddenly, with Sheriff Deace's truck out front along with another fire truck and a couple of deputy vehicles. I made sure my rifle was pointed somewhere safe, but in such an attitude that I could get it back into action fast, as Pipes and I walked up to where Deace was leaning over his truck's hood.

He looked up as we approached, and his eyes lit with relief. "There you are. Been wondering, but I didn't have a good way to get in touch with you in all this chaos."

"I got tied up killing some monsters in the diner." I looked around at the murk and the darkened hospital. "I gather things have gotten interesting out here?"

"You could say that." He nodded toward the dark bulk of the hospital behind him. "Still trying to get some backup generators going. The main backup got hit by a lightning strike. It's fried." He was looking at me with a raised eyebrow as he said it, and I shook my head. I didn't think it was a coincidence, either.

"Any other activity?" I realized that I'd gotten a bit too comfortable, mentioning monsters when I'd explained where I'd been. Not everyone can take this side of reality with equanimity. I didn't doubt that there were a fair number of Deace's deputies and other first responders who'd seen some pretty creepy stuff that day, but had explained it away. Most people do that.

He looked over his shoulder, as if he were trying to make sure there was no one nearby to overhear. "Seen some pretty weird stuff in the fog." He looked at Pipes. "The dark and the storm can make the mind play tricks on you, though, so I'm not sure what all I saw."

"It wasn't the storm playing tricks on us, Sheriff," Pipes said earnestly. "I don't know what those things were, but they were small, they were ugly, and they didn't go down until this guy came in throwing around holy water and praying in Latin."

Deace raised his eyebrows and gave a slight shrug that seemed to say, *Okay, then.* "Well, we've seen some little things that kind of hopped or skipped, but never close enough to see them clearly. Other critters that looked like coyotes or something, except they were running around on their hind legs."

I didn't recognize the description, but that there are lycanthropic Otherworlders that tended more toward the fox or the coyote than the wolf. They tended to be more of the sneaky, trickster, stab-in-the-back sorts than the brute force horror of the werewolf types.

I say *werewolf*, but most of them aren't really human, at least not to begin with.

"Any actual attacks?"

"Not on people, not that I know of, but there's been a rash of fires, and power and phones are both out for the whole town." He turned his eyes back to the map. "We've got radios, and that's about it. And we need 'em right now."

Almost on cue, the radio crackled. "Leutenburg Fire, Dispatch."

I'd been around first responders enough to know that on a night as busy as this seemed to be, that meant that Dispatch was losing track of which assets were available. That wasn't good.

"Dispatch, Engine Twenty-Twenty-Seven."

"Engine Twenty-Twenty-Seven, we have a radio report of a car just went off the road on Highway Three. Caller reports that it is upside down in the ditch just north of Seventh Street."

"That's right at the edge of town." Deace looked up with a frown, even as Engine Twenty-Twenty-Seven acknowledged. A moment later, before anyone could move, another call came in.

"Leutenburg Fire, Dispatch." The young lady on the radio was sounding increasingly haggard.

"Dispatch, Twenty-Twelve." The firefighter sounded almost as tired. And the night was far from over.

"I have another report of a rollover, Highway Three, this time just south of First Street."

I looked over at Deace, who had gone pale. "That's on the other side of town, isn't it?"

He nodded. "Any other day, I'd think it was a coincidence. But two people wrecking while they try to leave town, with the rest of this going on, after that freaky thing was in the old asylum? Nope. I'm not taking *anything* as a coincidence today."

I'd actually lost track of the fact that it was still daytime in all the dark and chaos. I glanced at my watch. Sunset wasn't for a few more hours.

More flashing lights sped through the fog toward the newest wreck. The fire department wasn't even bothering with sirens anymore. Hardly anyone wanted to be out on the streets in those conditions, and those who had dared it were already paying the price.

I scanned the veil of gray that had turned everything past the circle of flashing red and blue lights to shadows, my eyes narrowed, thinking. I didn't doubt that this storm was brought on because of the thing that I was hunting. This sort of thing usually meant that—depending on what it was—it was either showing the locals who was boss, or it was using the storm to cover for another attack. But who or what was the target?

While it was true that regular, rational tactical thinking didn't always apply to the Otherworld, sometimes you just had to start somewhere. And if I could go by what Deace had told me already, this thing had consistently acted like a human killer, just with Otherworldly abilities.

Unfortunately, I hadn't found a pattern that might suggest who the predator might be going after next. Leutenburg might be a small town, but finding a single target in a town of a few thousand people before the predator does, when you're groping in the dark, is next to impossible.

For a few seconds, as Deace tried to coordinate some more of the response to the accidents, while also telling his deputies to get ready to defend the town while trying not to get too specific about the threat, I just listened for screams, or anything else that might indicate where the predator was heading.

There was still a lot of noise, though, despite the fact that the thunder and lightning had stopped. That thing could be tearing someone to pieces on the other side of town and I'd never hear a thing.

Deace stepped up beside me while I was woolgathering. "Are you thinking what I'm thinking?"

"I'm no mind reader, Sheriff." It might have been curt, but I was tired, drenched, battered, and knew that I wasn't going to get to rest any time soon. That might have eroded my Christian charity a bit.

Fortunately, Deace didn't take offense. "I s'pose that's fair." He gusted a sigh. "I'm thinking that all of this is only the cover. The smokescreen, if you will. Chaos to keep us hopping while someone—or some*thing*—else does what they want to do."

"You're probably right." I was still watching the mists. Had I seen a shadow pop out from behind the hospital, as if it were peering at us, then duck back? I couldn't be sure. "Trouble is figuring out the who, what, and where." The "why" was currently irrelevant.

"Well, if you want to get in with me, I need to go around and check on things anyway." Deace jerked a thumb toward his truck. "Frankly, I'd be a lot more comfortable dealing with anything that might come up if you're along for the ride. We're a little out of our depth here."

"Sounds like a plan." To be honest, I didn't have a better one at the moment. I was still no closer to finding our quarry, and with the sheriff along, I wouldn't have to answer so many questions if I did need to intervene.

We climbed into his truck, and he started it up with a rumble. I had my Winchester across my knees, ready to get it pointed out the window in a heartbeat. It didn't look like the shadows in the mist were actively attacking people or vehicles at the moment. Taking out that little shaman seemed to have had a chilling effect on the Otherworlders.

We cruised down Main Street, which turned into Highway Three at either end. A few fires still guttered inside shattered storefront windows, but things had calmed down a bit, and wisps of fog drifted across the street in the sheriff's headlights.

He turned down one of the side streets, close to the edge of town. I could see the flickering red glow of fire department lights through the fog a little farther down the main drag, where one of the engines was seeing to the overturned car. I hoped that nobody tried to leave town again before we got this figured out. I didn't think that those wrecks were accidents any more than Deace did.

The gloom deepened as we moved down the street. No fires here. There seemed to be more movement, though. I thought I saw a shadow flit across the street, moving from house to house. It wasn't a drifting finger of mist. But it was gone before I could get a good enough look at it to figure out if it even needed to be shot, let alone bring my rifle to bear.

A Winchester 1886 wasn't the greatest firearm to be trying to wield from a truck window, either.

Deace gasped, and I looked up, just in time to see a toweringly tall figure, all darkness and shadow except for a pair of glowing, lambent eyes laden with malice, step out from behind a nearby house. It looked at us under what looked like the brim of a shady hat, then turned away, almost contemptuously, and strode down the street, now only a darker silhouette against the gloom.

"Follow that thing." Deace stared at me with some disbelief, but I held firm, my Winchester clasped in both hands. I couldn't tell him why I knew we had to follow the shadow man, at least not in any way that would satisfy his curiosity.

The truth was, I wasn't sure myself. This kind of war is more spiritual than physical, and sometimes there are nudges, from sources you can never be sure of. I suspected I knew, because this didn't feel like I should be dreading what was coming. You get attuned sometimes. Not that you get some sort of super sense when you take up the cross. You just get an occasional tap on the shoulder.

The sheriff was still looking at me like he wondered if I was crazy. "Just trust me." I shrugged. "You trusted me in that asylum with the owl-witch."

He still watched me for a second, glancing forward to make sure he wasn't about to drive off the road, then he shrugged in turn. "Yeah, I guess I did. Guess I just don't get how you know the things you know."

"Some of it's experience. Some of it is…other things."

He sighed again, shaking his head as he gripped the wheel with both hands and got us moving after the dark colossus striding down the street ahead of us. "I guess I'll take your word for it."

I didn't say anything. I'm not the most reassuring of men at the best of times, and this wasn't the best of times.

Especially as I realized, based on the map study of the town that I'd done, where that big shadow was going.

"Slow down. Don't lose it, but slow down. Let it get some distance." I really didn't want to go charging into Riddle's backyard, not if my suspicions were true.

"Why?" Deace might trust me, but he still needed more than that, especially when it came to tactical decisions.

"That thing's heading for the place you called the old Dermody house. I have my suspicions about Harper Riddle, and if that's going to meet him, then things are going to get real dangerous, real fast."

"They're already pretty damned dangerous," Deace pointed out.

I gritted my teeth. This was going to sound nuts, but Deace needed to understand. "I suspect that Riddle is involved in sorcery." At his look, I raised my eyebrows. "You've seen an owl-witch, a freak storm come up from nowhere full of monsters, and you're balking at the idea of *sorcery*?"

He turned back forward, his eyes wide. "I guess when you put it that way…"

We were coming to the edge of town. The Dermody house was on a sprawling estate just outside the city limits, set back in a draw in the bluffs that hemmed Leutenburg in. The shadow man was still moving that way.

Of course, in the tactical world, we always like to say that the enemy always gets a vote. When that enemy is from the Otherworld or the Abyss, that vote can get mighty weird.

The towering shadow paused, turned and glared at us over its shoulder, and then vanished like a popped soap bubble.

Deace started violently, but I put out a hand to steady him. "Don't get too rattled. They like that."

I was scanning the dark. The fog had really set in along the way to the Dermody house, though it wasn't a solid wall. Fingers of mist drifted back and forth, and it was darker than it should be. I glanced at my watch. *Way* darker than it should be.

Yeah, there was weirdness afoot on the Dermody place.

"Park here." I was actually a little late. Deace kept rolling a few yards and the engine died. He turned pale, but I just grimaced. *Here we go.*

I pushed my door open, pausing to turn to the sheriff. "You can stay here if you'd rather not deal with what's in there, Sheriff. It's no reflection on you. You weren't trained for this." I'd gotten the training after poking my nose into things that were better left alone, but I'd still gotten it. Deace was in over his head, he knew it, and he was scared stiff.

But he wasn't going to shirk. He probably thought that he couldn't look himself in the mirror anymore if he stayed back and let me go in there. "No, I'm coming with you." He pushed his door open, dragging a shotgun out with him.

I got my feet on the ground. It was bitingly cold in the swirling mist, which was far from what the weather had been like before the storm. I didn't think the drop in temperature was a natural outgrowth of the rain and hail, either.

The noises echoing down that draw from the Dermody house only strengthened my doubts. Those screams, wails, and a strange, eerie whistle didn't belong to anything natural.

"Hold your fire unless I tell you to shoot." I was almost more nervous about having a scared sheriff at my back with a shotgun than I was about confronting whatever Riddle had summoned. I paused, as much as it went against the grain to turn away from the horror ahead. Not that I was enamored of the fear and the weirdness, but it had been beaten into me a long time ago never to take your eyes off the threat. But this had to be done.

I looked Deace in the eyes. Fortunately, while he was staring wide-eyed into the murk ahead, hearing the monster movie noises, he turned to me as I warned him to keep his finger off the trigger. "Listen, Sheriff. This is your jurisdiction, but this kind of thing is my bailiwick. If you want to get out of this with your life—and your soul—intact, I suggest you do exactly what I tell you, when I tell you." I wished I had an exorcist along for this, but with the local priest based out of town, fifty miles away, that wasn't going to happen, especially if Riddle's fun and games had taken out the phones.

Not to mention those wrecks at the edge of town. I doubted anyone was getting in or out until this was over, either.

Deace might have gotten his back up under any other circumstances, hearing that from a stranger who'd just walked into town and almost gotten arrested. But he just nodded, a little shakily. "After what I've seen over the last twelve hours, you're not getting any argument from me. Lead on."

Turning back toward the drifting shreds of fog, I gritted my teeth, made the sign of the cross, and started in.

Chapter 12

If anything, it got even darker as we moved up the road. In my previous life, I would have done my utmost to stay off that dirt road, because that was where ambushes and IEDs tended to be set. Against the things in the fog, though, that didn't matter. I knew they were already entirely aware that I was there.

From the sounds of things, they were just more concerned with Riddle at the moment.

Glass shattered with a crash and a howl in the dark up ahead. Something up there wasn't happy. The low, moaning roar that followed chilled the blood, and somehow I was sure that it had come from that tall, slouch-hatted shadow we'd followed partway there. The *boom* that followed sounded like something massive hitting the side of a house.

I wanted to offset and find some cover in the worst way, and from the way he was stutter-stepping, so did Deace. "Cover and concealment won't do squat against these things, and if we try to find somewhere nice and dark to hide, we're probably going to get jumped by something with lots of claws and teeth that can fold itself into a crack in a boulder." I kept moving forward. "Straight up the middle is about our only real option here."

"Great." He didn't sound thrilled. I could relate. I wasn't thrilled, either.

There was a rail fence lining each side of the road, with grass on the other side, and trees that might have been willows hanging over the edges just ahead. I slowed down even more, my Winchester pointed at those trees, wondering if we'd made enough of an impression yet to get jumped here.

We had, but the expected swarm of monsters or swooping, howling assault from something worse didn't materialize.

Instead, a sepulchral voice echoed out of the fog, rising over the cacophony closer to the house. "This does not concern you, Witch Hunter."

"Afraid I'm going to have to beg to differ on that one," I said, momentarily proud that my voice didn't crack or shake. I didn't know what that thing was out there, but it was potent, I was sure of that. Worse, I didn't think it was our quarry, either. "This looks and sounds exactly like it's the kind of thing that's my concern." I had paused in the roadway, just before passing between the two nearest trees. "You're not supposed to be here."

What might have been a low, earthshaking snarl came from the darkness. "I have walked these hills for countless years, mortal. Who are you to say where *I* belong? Who is this would-be medicine man, who tries to bind me to his will?"

"I couldn't care less about him," I replied, more cheerfully than I felt. "But I come in the Name of One greater than you or me, and I know you don't dare try to cross Him."

The voice was turning more feral, more savage, almost a growl. "This one called upon me. I have a right to deal with him."

That could mean a couple of things, and it made the hair on the back of my neck go up even farther than it already was. The demons of the Abyss often asserted legal rights to those who dabbled in their domain, and I'd narrowly escaped just such a claim, myself, some time back.

That said, there were powerful Otherworlders that could be just as legalistic, with actually fewer constraints than the demons had. The Otherworld was almost as in-between as the mortal world, and I'd found some of those creatures that lived in that in-between that had thrown their lot in with Heaven. It was rare, but it did happen, whereas the demons were inveterate enemies of the Most High and everyone and everything that He had ever created, from now to eternity.

Before I could answer, though, the thing in the mist apparently decided that the conversation was over.

A thundered command came out of the dark and the fog, a word that was in no human language. My head immediately started to hurt, and Deace staggered, putting a hand to his nose. It came away bloody.

There was no time to see to him. With a thunder of hoofs and a squealing series of bleats, four goatheads came charging out of the dark, their heads down and their grasping hands held out as they tried to close the distance before I could get my rifle into action.

That wasn't all that off brand for goatheads. They're not very smart. They're also not really so far into the Otherworld that they need special rounds to kill them.

I blasted the first one through the brisket, and it stopped in its tracks, went a little higher on its hoofs, and dropped onto its face. The other three hesitated, but another booming, unearthly command drove them forward again.

That split-second hesitation gave me the opening I needed, as I quickly levered another round into the chamber and shot a second. The third one took a massive, 405-grain bullet through the teeth a second later, and then Deace blasted the last one with his 12 gauge. It wasn't what I'd told him to do, but at that point, I wasn't in a good position to chew him out over it. He'd watched his fire and he'd hit what he'd been aiming at.

I almost expected a freakout about what those things had been, but Deace kept it together. He'd seen freakier stuff than goatheads over the last day or so, after all. In comparison to an owl-witch, a sorcerous storm out of nowhere, and that massive shadow figure, goatheads were pretty tame.

He was still muttering to himself. I couldn't make out most of it, as the wind started to pick up again, and I thought that I could hear some incantation being chanted over the unearthly hooting and howling in the dark up ahead, but I could recognize the tone.

Anywhere else, Deace would be contemplating finding a different, quieter place to work. Unfortunately for him, there was no such place where this sort of thing was concerned.

Stepping around the sprawled, twitching bodies of the goatheads, which were already starting to break down—the Otherworld is a bit unstable when it steps into the "light" of the regular world—I continued to advance toward the Dermody house. I was praying as I shoved more rounds into the Winchester's tube. I didn't know what that shadow thing was, but it was potent, and fighting it was not going to be fun.

And that was leaving aside the fact that a lot of the noise seemed to have started before that thing showed up.

The fog was getting thicker, though it felt simultaneously clammy and grimy, as if it were a combination of dust, smoke, and mist. That told me all I needed to know; this wasn't just weather.

As if that was still a question at that point.

I wasn't sure what we were going to face next, but I can't say I was expecting to get about ten paces before I found we weren't alone.

My rifle pivoted toward the figure crouched atop a fencepost as soon as I realized it was there, but I held my fire. I couldn't say right in the moment *why*, except that sometimes shooting first doesn't work all that well against something that's not entirely susceptible to bullets.

The shadowy figure that we had followed was perched on the fencepost like a vulture, its body—if it really had such a thing—wrapped in a cloak of shadow. Its hat shaded its face, while its eyes had turned more green than red as they stared at us out of the darkness.

Deace swore, but he was still collected enough that he followed my lead and held his fire.

For a long moment, while the eerie noises continued to echo from the direction of the house, the spook and I stared back at each other. While it didn't speak right away, I still sensed that something had fundamentally changed. And it went deeper than the shift in color in its glowing eyes.

"I cannot touch you, Witch Hunter." The sepulchral voice seemed almost petulant. "You would take my prey away from me, though he has cast himself out of the protection your Master affords."

"Doesn't matter. I've got business with him." I wasn't going to elaborate with this thing. I still didn't think it was the predator I was looking for—I wasn't getting that kind of feeling from it—but it was dangerous, that much I was sure of. Yet the fact that it was talking was interesting.

"Which means you can either try me—and by extension, the One who sent me—or you can walk."

While I spoke, I could feel Deace's eyes on me. He was probably wondering why I was talking with this thing instead of shooting it in the face, but I had my reasons.

The fact that it was talking instead of coming after us hammer and tongs, coupled with its insistence that it was only interested in Riddle, told me something. This wasn't a demon—sure, they could be deceptive, but it had come to talk to a Witch Hunter, knowing who was probably waiting in the wings nearby—so it was an Otherworlder of some persuasion. What kind, I didn't know, but something powerful enough that Riddle had tried to bind it by invocation yet not so powerful that it would attempt to face the silver cross with outright hostility.

"A debt has been incurred." The voice deepened, some of the snarl coming back. "He sought to bind me, to drag me forth as a weapon." Something almost like anguish came into those hollow tones. "Is my punishment already not enough?"

That brought me up short a little. There were stories about Otherworlders who had changed sides but still needed to atone for what they had done. The rules for such things are different for them than they are for either angels or men. They are somewhere in between, and thus the rules get hazy for those without a direct line to On High.

I could be said to have more of a direct line than some, but that hardly put me on St. Peter's confidant list. And some things we're just not supposed to inquire too deeply into.

"He's got a heavier debt that I'm here to collect," I replied. I might be surprised that this spook was talking to me, and that it might be one of those Otherworlders that was cursed to walk the Earth until the end for something it had actually repented of, but I had my own job to do, and the silver crucifix around my neck meant that my mission outranked whatever debt of honor this thing might have. "I'll say it again. You can step aside, or this can get unpleasant." I tilted my head slightly to one side. "If you really are walking off your penance, you might want to think twice about crossing a Witch Hunter."

It might have snarled. If it really was working off a long punishment in anticipation of the end times, then it wouldn't want to cross me—more accurately, it wouldn't want to cross the Power behind me—but even repentant Otherworlders still weren't angels or saints. There was a lot of passion wrapped up with considerable power over the natural world there, and it was angry and frustrated.

"*He sought to chain me again!*" There was real anguish in that cry, one amplified by unearthly means to the point that the sheer volume of it almost made me stagger.

"And what do you think is gonna happen if you get between me and him?" I might be able to sympathize, as much as that was possible when dealing with an Otherworldly monster, but my responsibility was far more important than its vendetta, no matter how justified it might be. "Face it. This isn't a fight you're going to win. Either way."

It could still rip my head off, and it had tried with those goatheads. But if it was *really* concerned with some sort of penance, doing that wasn't going to count in its favor in the long run.

Some Otherworlders have a high sense of justice and the binding force of debts. Many of them use it against mere mortals, often for their own amusement, though sometimes out of a more alien thought process than most people can grasp. I didn't honestly know which was the case here, and while it might *seem* sincere, you could never really trust an Otherworlder.

For the most part. There *were* exceptions, but they were generally the exceptions that proved the rule.

It straightened, though it was still perched on that fence post, so that it now towered nearly fifteen feet in the air. It glared down at me with those blazing green points of fire, the dimness of the cloud-shrouded sky above blacked out by the spreading brim of its hat.

Every instinct told me to lift my rifle as it stood there, but while I might not know what this shadowy figure was, something told me that even the iron or silver rounds I carried wouldn't do much against it. This thing was old and powerful, and, standing face to face with it, I didn't have the time to figure out how to drive it back underground, except by sheer force of the authority I held as a member of the Order of the Silver Cross.

So, I kept my rifle cradled in the crook of my arm, lifted the crucifix in my shooting hand, and began to pray the St. Michael prayer. This creature might not be a demon, but having the Captain on my side was going to be a help, regardless.

He wasn't always solely focused on the threats from the Abyss.

The implicit threat did the trick. The thing seemed to clench fists of smoky blackness at its side, threw its head back, and screamed. The sound was a terrible thunder, and it drove Deace to his knees. I staggered a little, though I fought to keep myself upright, struggling not to turn my eyes away.

I thought I felt a hand at my back, steadying me. *Thanks*, I thought. The hand might have gripped my shoulder, then it was gone as I steadied myself.

At the same moment, as the peal of thunder that was the old spook's howl died away, it vanished as thoroughly as if it had never been there.

The screams and howls died away, though the fog clung to the draw, and there was still a gritty, clammy sense of evil there. What Riddle had been doing I could only guess.

I had to hope that he hadn't gone so far that I was going to have to call in an exorcist before we did anything else.

Helping Deace to his feet, making sure he still had his shotgun, my own Winchester held ready again, I started to advance deeper into the darkness, toward the Dermody place.

Chapter 13

The house was old, all right. It had been renovated, but the hallmarks of 19th century architecture were there. It actually looked a little out of place, or it would have if I hadn't seen a dozen other weird, gothic mansions built by eccentric millionaires in small towns across the West.

I was moving up the fence along the driveway, and Deace had shifted to do the same on the other side of the path, his shotgun held ready, though even in the gloom, I could tell he was pale and sweating. The dispersion and tactical approach weren't going to do anything but keep us from accidentally shooting each other if the monsters came out of the fog, but what else were we going to do?

That Deace was moving that way told me that he'd had some other training before he'd been sheriff.

There were still whispers in the dark, though the real cacophony had died away as the shadow creature had departed. There was something else, too, almost a low chanting or some sort of music, the kind of creepy stuff that put my teeth on edge, even when it wasn't explicitly invocative.

It got louder as we got closer, confirming my hunch that it wasn't something sorcerous or Otherworldly, coming from the mists. It was a recording, inside the house. And as we got closer, and mounted the steps to the porch, it became clearer that it was some sort of deliberately creepy haunted house music. Maybe some horror movie soundtrack. I couldn't be sure.

As kind of pitiful as it was, it told me something. And it made the night's horrors that much worse.

I didn't think I was dealing with someone who really knew what they were doing, as bad as that would have been. I seemed to be dealing with an amateur occult dabbler, and he was about as safe to be around as a toddler with a shotgun.

Even if the Otherworldly killer I was hunting wasn't bad enough, these sorts of amateurs tend to give openings to creatures much, much worse.

I hesitated just outside the door, remembering a conversation with something that chose to look like an urbane, sophisticated man with a pointed beard, something as old as the universe itself, and possessed of a malice to match. Professor Ashton hadn't set out to summon Mephistopheles, but he'd attracted the old devil's attention, nevertheless.

Riddle might have just made the situation here in Leutenburg that much worse.

I crossed myself and kicked in the door.

Deace didn't object to my breaking and entering without announcing myself, or allowing him to do it. That set him apart from a few sheriffs I'd dealt with over the years, but I figured that after everything else he'd seen lately, he was in survival mode.

The entryway was dark, smoke drifting from recently extinguished candles. There were little plaques with sigils cut into them that made the eyes smart to look at them. I knocked them down as I passed. I'd deal with them later.

There was a smell on the air, mostly smoke but with some of that burned-blood scent that always seemed to go along with sorcery.

We paced down the hallway, toward the living room in the back of the house. The music was louder, and just as obnoxious, though it lacked the truly horrifying tones that might have really contributed to whatever ritual he'd just attempted. More candle smoke drifted through the darkened house, and I heard movement and then a crash and a curse. It was almost as if all the candles had blown out at once.

Deace had a flashlight on his shotgun, and I'd held mine clamped to the forearm of my rifle since just before making entry. They cast cones of white light, crossed by drifting tendrils of smoke, as we moved carefully toward the living room.

My light stabbed across the hall and pinned Riddle, wearing black robes and a stole with occult symbols embroidered on it, where he'd tripped and fallen in the dark. He squinted against the glare, holding up a hand to shield his eyes as Deace and I entered the room.

I swept the rest of the place with my light and my rifle muzzle, while Deace stayed focused on Riddle. That wasn't ideal; maybe he hadn't been quite as well trained as I'd thought, but then, maybe he figured I was better equipped to deal with any creepy crawlies that came out of the shadows, and he wasn't willing to turn away from Riddle now that he had him pinned down.

There were windows in the living room, but they'd been covered by dark hangings, though they all looked like they'd been room darkening blinds, rather than the mysterious tapestries that Riddle probably would have wanted. The whole place was lit only by our weapon lights.

Despite the fact that he was being blinded by our flashlights, Riddle seemed to know exactly who we were. "No, no, no, *what have you done?!*" He wasn't just scared, he was screaming in all-out, out-of-his-mind panic. He was looking around the room at the smoking candles, and something on the table that was smoking a bit more than the suddenly-extinguished tapers.

I wasn't sure I wanted to know *what* was smoking on that table, given the symbols he'd painted on the top around it.

He was staring at me, not at Deace, despite the fact that our lights should have made it impossible to tell which of us was which, since we were both pointing our cones of illumination at his face. *"You ruined everything! Why did you do that? Do you know what he's going to do to me now!?"* His face was twisted with passion and terror.

Before I could even try to calm him down, he snatched an ornamental knife out of his robes and lunged at me.

If I'd had more time, I would have sighed. Why did they always have to make this hard? My finger tightened on the trigger, not without some regret.

I've had to kill a few sorcerers and witches. The kind of dabblers who have sold their souls and opened the way for the monsters and the demons to wreak as much havoc as possible. For the most part, the demons want people corrupted *before* they die, but if they can find enough corruption already there—and there's more than enough to go around these days—then they'll gladly fuel mass murder, knowing that they'll have a claim on the dead wholesale. That makes the summoners and channelers a clear and present danger to temporal as well as eternal life of innocent—or not-so-innocent, but that's part of the point—people around them.

That didn't mean I relished it. There'd been a time, and there were still characters and situations that I wouldn't mourn, but my job was that of a protector, and as a man of

God, I had to seek other people's redemption, first and foremost. "Love your enemies, do good to those who hate you." Sometimes, though, there really was no other choice.

This wasn't one of those times, it turned out. Just before my trigger broke, Riddle locked up and fell on his face, twitching. I could hear the snapping of Deace's taser as I let off the pressure on the trigger, whispering a silent prayer of thanks that I hadn't needed to blow Riddle's head off.

Lowering my rifle, I still covered the would-be sorcerer while Deace got his handcuffs out. "Thanks for not killing him." Deace had slung his shotgun, the light setting shadows dancing crazily around the room, though he still had the taser in his hand, as he hit it again when Riddle tried to move. The robed man jerked and twitched, and Deace kicked the knife away from his hand. "Harper Riddle, you're under arrest for attempted murder." The sheriff looked up at me. "Not sure I could have arrested him for weird Halloween stuff, though from what I've seen I probably should have. Just don't think a judge would necessarily believe any of it."

He wasn't wrong. I'd run into clergy who didn't believe this stuff until it stared them in the face, and sometimes not even then. Judges really weren't inclined to believe that anything beyond the normal of their own experience was real.

As he released the taser and started to handcuff Riddle, the would-be sorcerer arched his back and looked up at me, his teeth gritted, and started to chant something.

I didn't wait for Deace. Stepping in close, I put the muzzle of my Winchester against Riddle's forehead. "None of that."

He shut up fast, his eyes crossing as he tried to focus on the massive octagonal barrel hovering entirely too close to his precious personal skull for his comfort. Deace glanced at me, then looked down at Riddle as the handcuffs snicked closed. "You have the right to remain silent, Mr. Riddle. I suggest you use it."

I almost said something, but then I looked at the wild look in Riddle's eyes as he stared at me, unblinking, half panicked, and realized that any information I got out of him was going to necessarily be suspect. Whatever he was up to in Leutenburg, he wasn't on our side.

"Keep an eye on him." I didn't want to have to go into detail, but I didn't need Riddle trying to summon demons or monsters, or trying to cast curses while I went to work. I looked around with a grimace. "This is going to take a minute, and you still might want to keep this place taped off as a crime scene for a while." I pulled the holy water flask out of my back pocket. Riddle started to thrash and snarl, and Deace dropped a knee into the small of his back to keep him down.

"Should we just burn it down?" It was probably the first time I'd ever heard a law enforcement officer suggest some cleansing arson, but it wasn't all that wild an idea, either.

I shook my head as I shook holy water in the sign of the cross over the first of the little plaques there in the room. The air seemed to tense, and Riddle let out a low moan, almost more a sound of despair and fear than anger. "Not necessarily. Infestation can be a problem for a while, but places can be cleansed more easily than people can." The next plaque fell over as I sprinkled holy water on it, and Riddle flinched, as the temperature in the room seemed to drop a couple of degrees. I realized as I worked—knowing that I was going to have to contact the local priest and get him to come do this more thoroughly—that I couldn't hear the storm anymore, and the screaming and howling outside had completely died away. The old Dermody house was dead silent except for Riddle's squirming.

It took a little time to work my way all the way around the room, dousing each occult item with holy water, praying a deliverance prayer under my breath the whole time. Riddle stayed quiet, though I could feel his eyes on me as I worked. Occasionally, I heard a hiss or a snarl as the holy water hit a plaque or a medallion, or some other dark talisman. Sometimes they fell over, sometimes they smoked, sometimes they got really energetic, and flipped into the air or cracked in half. Whatever Riddle had been up to, he'd gotten his grubby mitts on some pretty potent cursed artifacts. That made me wonder about my theory that he was a dangerous amateur. He'd put a *lot* of work into this operation, and he'd done some serious digging to prep for it. I glanced at him where he was staring, wondering how much of his reaction was an act.

By the time I was finished, he wasn't putting up a fight anymore. He was limp under Deace, though the sheriff wasn't taking any chances and kept his weight on him.

I came back over and squatted down in front of Riddle, my Winchester back in the crook of my arm. I nodded to Deace, who stood up, though not before kicking the knife away. Understandably, he didn't seem to want to touch it or pick it up, after what he'd seen happen with a bunch of Riddle's other stuff.

"Harper Riddle." My voice was a bit of a harsh croak at that point. I'd already been through a couple of nasty scrapes, I hadn't slept in over twenty-four hours, and, frankly, I wasn't happy. "As the sheriff said, you have the right to remain silent. From a temporal legal perspective, that's probably the smart thing to do. If you hadn't tried to stab me right in front of the sheriff, you could even get off scot free, in this life, anyway. Granted, it also wasn't that smart when I could have put a .45-70 through your skull from about six feet." I shook my head. He still had his head down, his forehead resting on the floor. "Look at me, Riddle." I let some of that old Marine edge into my voice.

Apparently, he was so beaten that he didn't even think of fighting me anymore. He looked up, his eyes bleary, as Deace started to pull aside the curtains, letting some light into the room. The fog was gone and the clouds were starting to disperse outside. The storm really was over.

"Do you have any idea what you've done?" His hoarse whisper positively dripped with despair.

"What *I've* done?" I almost laughed. "Riddle, you really are out of your depth." Any mirth vanished from my voice. "What were you trying to do? Are you working for the thing that's been murdering people here for a century?" I was going to have some very pointed questions for him if that was the case. Not that I could necessarily expect him to tell the truth about it at first, anyway.

"No!" He looked up at me, and the desperation in his eyes seemed sincere enough. "No, I really am trying to help."

Deace laughed bitterly. "Some help. Monsters all over town, fires, car wrecks. I'd hate to see what you think an attack looks like."

"Let me guess. You thought you'd summon that shadowman to help you." I shook my head again. "Except he got pissed when you tried to bind him and showed up with all of his little minions to rip your head off. Otherworlders tend to be touchy about things like that, and if you don't know what you're doing, they'll take you out in a heartbeat. Of course, if you *do* know what you're doing, you're in even worse trouble, but most idiots like you don't tend to take that into consideration until it's far too late." My voice got hard again. "Who did you invoke to bind him, Riddle?"

He looked down at the floor again. *"Answer me, Riddle."* I had my suspicions, given the horrors out in the rest of town. The shadowman had been after Riddle himself. It was *possible* that he'd sent more minions after the whole town. I'd seen Otherworlders get immensely destructive in fits of pique. But it hadn't felt like that, not when I'd spoken with the creature. And those little goblin things in the diner had been trying to summon something else.

He still didn't look at me, but he whispered a name. A name that almost made me cough, and Deace, despite not knowing what it signified, recoiled. Sometimes things of the Abyss instill a certain instinctive revulsion, unless you've gone so far down the wrong path that you've become desensitized.

"You moron." I straightened up. I wasn't familiar with the name in question, but that didn't mean much. Sometimes these things use different names, sometimes they make them up on the spot. But the instinctive reaction was enough.

"He was going to tell me what the killer was and how to defeat it!" He was getting defensive, which was pretty standard, and also pretty dumb. It wasn't as if there was a plethora of evidence that he had been dabbling in things best not messed with. And when you think that playing around with the obviously evil stuff is somehow going to be defensible, you've already lost the plot.

"Sure, he was. And then, when you found yourself outclassed and being hunted, he'd leave you to your fate, because you've already created a relationship with him, and—whatever he says—that relationship really only goes one way." I shook my head again.

"Well, now he's definitely going to come for me, because of *you!*" He almost screamed it, sobbing as he looked around at the ruin I'd made of his ceremonial room. "The deal was made! Now he's going to come to collect!"

I sighed. "That's not really how this works. He *can't* come to 'collect,' as you put it, until you die. Not without finding some way to manifest in the physical world, and that's tougher than it sounds." I'd seen it happen, but it was rare. I didn't think whatever small-time demon Riddle had made a deal with would be able to do it, not without some considerable change in the metaphysical terrain in Leutenburg.

Of course, there might still be something I was missing.

I straightened, looking down at Riddle, crying in fear on the floor. He'd screwed around with forces best left alone, and now he was terrified of the consequences. He didn't realize how fortunate he was that I'd intervened when I had.

Of course, that might all still be for nothing if he didn't turn his life around. But that was something that he had to decide to do on his own.

As long as he wasn't actively summoning demons or monsters—or trying to curse or kill people—then I had to keep my hands off. Being a Witch Hunter can be a bit like being a cop, except dealing with weirder stuff on a more regular basis.

"You done?" Deace asked. "I'd rather get him in a cell for now, unless you need more out of him."

"I'm done." I looked down at Riddle, but I couldn't just leave it at that. "You've got a choice ahead of you, Harper. You can turn away from all of this, walk away and never look back, or you can find yourself at the end, hearing the words, 'I never knew you,' at which point whatever nasty you've had the most dealings with is going to drag you down into the Abyss to have its way with you for an eternity. Think about it."

I couldn't tell if my words were getting through or not. He was still hanging his head, still crying quietly, not looking at me. Deace bent to put a hand under Riddle's armpit and pulled him to his feet. I stepped back, keeping my rifle ready, just in case.

Riddle didn't try anything, but I saw him glance at me from under his hanging hair as Deace pulled him toward the front door. My own eyes narrowed as they started out toward the road. Riddle didn't look back, though Deace did. I waved to indicate that I was going to look around some more, and Deace nodded, though I stayed where I was and watched them as they headed for Deace's truck.

There had been something in that look, something that had put a faint chill up my spine. I couldn't be sure, but I had the sudden hunch that the crying was just an act. That there was nothing repentant about Riddle, and that he was already on his Plan B.

That could be bad. For the moment, though, he was Deace's problem. Without his setup, he was less of a threat, unless he became fully possessed, and while that was possible, it wouldn't make him unstoppable. If he was locked up, possessed or not, he was going to stay that way unless someone—or something—broke him out.

That gave me a faint shudder as I turned back to the interior of the house. Riddle could still cause a lot of damage, if he was deeper than it had first appeared.

But, he might just point me in the right direction, too.

It was with considerable distaste that I started to search the house. There was a *lot* of creepy stuff. Most of it was glorified Hot Topic goth stuff, but there were still quite a few more genuine occult objects, some in display cases, some lying around on his desk or his kitchen table. I was careful to make the sign of the cross over each of them, even the tacky, relatively harmless looking ones, and was going to be running low on holy water by the time I was done in that house.

Finally, as it was genuinely getting dark outside, I found a notebook. It wasn't one of the fake leather "journals" or wannabe "grimoires," of which Riddle had plenty. It was an old, ratty college-ruled notebook, with the spotty cover and a simple "Notes" scrawled in Sharpie on the front.

I flipped through it, confirming my suspicions. As I did so, I suddenly felt a stir of air in the room, as if something big had moved, or a breath of wind had just passed through the closed house. That wasn't good.

Looking around, I made sure the silver crucifix was out on my chest. It was tempting to get confrontational, but that was temptation. I wasn't an exorcist, and there were very rare circumstances where I was in any position to go directly up against anything from the Abyss by myself.

Even in those circumstances, it was rarely a great idea.

It might grate on my pride to turn tail, so to speak, but that was temptation, too. Tucking the notebook under my arm, I got out of there. I had a bit of a hike back to town, but I wasn't staying in that house without an exorcist to back me up.

Chapter 14

The notebook was not pleasant reading. Riddle had been searching into a lot of really dark stuff, and the tone of his writing about some of the more occult killings he'd studied, not to mention the sorcery stuff, was a little too eager, a little too interested. There was an adolescent fascination in the way he described these things, not the sort of clinical attention that a scholar might use.

I didn't attempt to read it all in one go. A lot of it I just sort of skimmed, pausing from time to time to pray. Reading those notes made me feel like I needed to take a shower. Riddle hadn't seemed—at least so far—to get into some of the *really* dark stuff, but he was still dabbling with sorcery, and all the gross crap that goes along with it. As near as I could tell, at least by a couple weeks ago, judging by the dates on the notes, he hadn't advanced to ritual child abuse, but if he kept going the way he was going, it was only a matter of time.

He *was* trying to find the killer, that much was clear from his notes. Alongside the evil that seemed to leave a gritty, greasy film on my skin just from reading about it, there was a shocking naivete in his writing. This guy genuinely thought that invoking spirits and "energies" could be harnessed to some good end, despite the really sketchy stuff he was having to do to try and accomplish it. And he'd been doing a *lot* of sketchy stuff. He was deeper than I'd thought, that much was clear.

I put the notebook down and stepped outside, whispering a Pater Noster as I went. I looked up at the sky. It was night already—which might not be the best time to read occult garbage—but the clouds had mostly cleared out, leaving the stars shining brightly in the sky above.

No matter how dark things got, the clouds always cleared away eventually.

I didn't know why that thought had popped into my head. Maybe someone Up There thought I needed a reminder. Maybe I was just looking for some encouragement in the face of the horror that I'd seen, and that may have become worse with Riddle's meddling.

Headlights swung toward my campsite, and tires crunched in the gravel, the rumble of the engine driving away the quiet of the night. The truck looked familiar, especially as the driver killed the headlights, revealing Deace behind the wheel as he parked, shut off the engine, and pushed his door open.

"Got Riddle all tucked in?" I knew he was there to talk about our next move, and I wasn't sure I was ready to discuss it, yet. There was still more of the notebook to go through, as much as I didn't relish the thought.

"Yep." He came around to the front of his truck and leaned on the bumper, since I was doing the same on my tailgate. He folded his arms and studied me. "You find what you were looking for in there?"

"Maybe." I jerked a thumb over my shoulder. "Riddle was a note-taker. I found his journal—his *real* journal."

Deace leaned to one side to look past me into the truck. "Interesting reading?"

I snorted. "For certain values of the word. I do know that he was a genuine third party, and he wasn't working for our predator. He seems to have genuinely believed he was trying to hunt it down and stop it."

"He wasn't, though? Not really?" Deace still wasn't sure about all this weird stuff.

I rubbed a thumb along my jaw, thinking about how to put this. "Even if he'd clashed with the predator, the odds were pretty good that it and his 'new friends' would turn out to be on the same side. The rivalries in the Abyss and the Otherworld can get pretty intense, but they're also deceptive, and if any ordinary person starts to think that he's got things figured out, they change pretty quickly." I tapped the silver crucifix on my chest. "This is about the only loyalty or hostility you can count on. *Really* count on."

"So, if he'd managed to harness that shadowman, or whatever that thing was, it might still have turned on him and ripped his head off?"

"Maybe. Or it might have simply bent the knee to the stronger monster and let him get killed. No way to tell, without digging into histories that are hard to find and even harder to trust." I reached back, grabbed my water bottle, and took a swig. "There's a reason why people shouldn't get too fascinated with this weird stuff."

"Yet here you are." He was probing.

I laughed, softly and without much humor. "Yeah, here I am. Penance, I suppose you could say, for getting a bit too fascinated with the weird stuff."

He kept watching me, but I really wasn't interested in elaborating. That had been a dark time, and as much as I kept venturing into the shadows afterward, at least now I was, quite literally, on the side of the angels.

After a while, he sighed and spat into the dust, out in the dark. I wondered if my little visitor from before was still lurking out there. Probably not; I would have sensed it or heard something by now.

If anything, that silence worried me more than the harassment had. If the creepy crawlies in the dark weren't trying to make my life miserable, it generally meant that they wanted me to keep going down the road I was following, and that was never good.

Unfortunately, right at the moment, I didn't see any other options, aside from waiting until the predator struck again, and then trying to backtrack from the scattered body parts. I didn't think that was a great choice, either.

Deace wasn't looking at me anymore, but staring up at the stars in the sky above. Finally, he shook his head. "It's enough to make a man think about going back to church."

"I'd advise it." When he looked down at me, a little startled, I snorted. "What? You thought that the monster hunter with a silver crucifix around his neck was going to turn out to be some sort of agnostic?"

He chuckled faintly, though there was a tautness, a sense of lingering fear and horror in the sound. Deace had seen a lot in the last twenty-four hours, and none of it had been calculated to make him feel like the ground under him was particularly solid. "I guess you've got a point."

Silence fell. I kept glancing toward the shadows around the campsite and the river below. The quiet was getting on my nerves. Why had the things that go bump in the night stopped bumping?

I could only pray and keep going. That thing out there needed to be taken down, and I was the only one of the Order here.

Turning an eye to Deace, I raised an eyebrow. "Don't take this the wrong way, Sheriff, but I'd suggest you keep a close eye on Riddle."

"You don't think his scared and out of his depth act is sincere?" Deace seemed somewhat more comfortable talking about a perp than the strangeness he'd witnessed recently.

"Not really." I nodded toward my truck bed and the book that I was avoiding going back to. "He's been digging around in this stuff too long not to have a pretty good idea what he's been getting into. He might think he's drawn a line—I can't be sure, because I haven't gotten to the end yet—but that's always self-deception when it comes to this stuff. Sorcery's a bit like hard drugs. Once you start down that path, it gets harder and harder to turn back the farther you go."

"That's not encouraging." Deace winced a little. "I've had to deal with the hardcore addicts before."

"Well, not to discourage you even further, Sheriff, but this is actually a lot worse. Addicts don't tend to summon demons and monsters."

"Great." He shook his head with a sigh, looking down at the dirt. "So, what? I go back to the jail to watch our would-be witch doctor, and you go spook hunting on your own?"

"Afraid so." I shrugged. "I don't like it any more than you do, Sheriff. Hell, I probably like it less. But Riddle changed the calculations when he got froggy. We don't *know* that he failed completely. Those little goblin things in the diner were trying to bring something through, and they would have if I hadn't been there. Who knows what else got unleashed this afternoon? That storm covered the whole town and a good chunk of the hills around it."

"Don't you think that it would be a better idea for you to have backup?"

"You're still going to be my backup, Sheriff." I grinned at him like a skull. "By making sure that Riddle isn't up to any tricks to try to sic those things on me while I'm out hunting."

He sighed, then reached into his truck and pulled out a radio. "Well, at least take this, since I haven't seen you carry a phone. If you're out there in the coulees and get cornered, I won't know until it's too late, otherwise."

I took the radio. "If I get cornered out there, Sheriff, there probably isn't much you'll be able to do, but I appreciate it."

"Don't say that." He sighed and turned to his truck. "Well, happy reading, or hunting, or both. Just don't hesitate to call me if you do get into trouble."

"Don't worry, Sheriff." I waved as I started to climb back into the bed of my truck. "I don't intend to go looking tonight, anyway."

"I'm a bit more worried about what might be looking for you, to be honest. Keep that Winchester of yours handy."

"Always do."

***

I took another look at the notebook and weighed my options and priorities. A part of me really didn't want to continue reading, especially not in the dark, but all the same, the truth of what I'd said about the threat to the town from that attempted summoning was pressing on me. Riddle had raised the stakes, and even if he hadn't succeeded in what he'd been trying to do, there was no way that our quarry hadn't noticed.

And if it was as dangerous and powerful an Otherworlder as I thought it was—and few managed a hunt like this that spanned a century otherwise—it wouldn't be just sitting back and waiting for the other shoe to drop.

Gritting my teeth, saying another prayer, both for protection and perseverance, I dove back in.

I'd been right. Things did get worse.

I think I've found the key to the binding ritual. It kind of makes me a little queasy, but I've just got to get over that. No sorcerer ever reached greatness by balking when things get unpleasant. The art is dark by ordinary lights. And I have to think about what comes after. What can be accomplished.

It's a little strange. The Castaneda stuff worked, but this seems to be far beyond it. Not only in the extent to which I have to step outside my comfort zone, turn my back on the mundane and socially acceptable, but in what it has the potential to do.

I'd be lying if I said I wasn't scared. This is a huge step, and it goes against everything I was taught as a kid. But it's necessary if I'm going to keep becoming.

He'd underlined the word "becoming." I looked up, just to get my eyes off the page. I already knew what came next.

I won't repeat the descriptions on the next pages. Suffice it to say that he hadn't been kidding about, "going beyond the socially acceptable." He should be in prison.

A particularly savage part of my mind, one that I had to fight every day, thought that he really should be in the dirt.

After scanning the darkness around the truck, momentarily worried that just reading that had opened a door to the things in the dark, I reluctantly returned my attention to the pages. I skipped ahead, skimming in case there was anything that I needed to know, trying to force the images from the descriptions of ritual horror out of my head.

I had to finish this, because Riddle hadn't just come here on a hunch. While he'd referred to it obliquely during the rest of the notebook, he'd clearly had a target in mind from when he'd really gotten serious about sorcery. He'd known he was coming to Leutenburg for a while.

Now, as I got deeper in, things became clearer.

While the true nature of the Leutenburg Killer is still elusive, I think that I have found a way to find out more and gain an ally against it at the same time. There are old stories, going back to when the first ranchers settled in the area, about a shadowman that walks the hills. Seems to be less aggressive than the usual shadowman, but he's been there longer than the Killer. I think I've figured out all the invocations to bind a shadowman. It will be the toughest ritual I've tried so far, but if I can make it work...

I skipped past the calculations and plans for the ritual. I'd already crashed that party.

Then I found the jackpot. Maybe.

There aren't any real stories about the Leutenburg Killer. Interesting. Nobody wants to talk about it. So, I can't find any historical haunts that I might be able to research. I've been hiking the hills around town. Narrowly avoided getting shot for trespassing yesterday, but I think I might have found something.

There's a spot on the Collins farm, about a mile south of the house. Nobody goes there. None of the animals go there. Collins has it completely fenced off with no gate. I got close, despite his dogs, and while he wasn't around. There's a deep draw there, and there's a cave. None of the dogs wanted to get close, either, and I didn't see any sign that any animals had gotten close to it in a very long time. The ground was completely undisturbed, except for some strange marks that I couldn't make out.

I moved in close and got over the fence. It got dark and cold down in that draw pretty fast. The dogs barking got quiet, too. It was weird. My hackles went up. I couldn't tell if there was anything down there, and I think that if it had been there, I'd have been killed.

The cave is set into the wall of the cleft, and it goes down before it levels off. There are signs of fire down there, but no petroglyphs on the walls. What is down there are skulls. Lots of skulls. No other bones; just skulls.

I think I've found the Killer's lair.

Now I have to start the first rituals to learn what it is and begin to prepare for the confrontation. If I can defeat the Killer, bring it to heel, then not only will all my study and effort be worth it, but I will be well on the way to the level that I'm really looking to get to.

The next paragraph really made my blood run cold. The handwriting changed to a paragraph of abstract symbols. They didn't make my eyes smart, so they weren't occult glyphs, so they must be some kind of shorthand. What brought the dread was the fact that there was something in that cave that Riddle had seen fit to write about in code, just in case anyone else came across his notebook.

I put the notebook down, looking out past my tailgate into the darkness. What did he find in that cave that he didn't want to put down in plain text? He still didn't seem to be entirely certain what the predator was, but he'd clearly found something important.

I had someplace to look. It was more than I'd had an hour ago, though the way I'd gotten the information still made me a little queasy. I'd have to move carefully.

Despite the urgency of the situation, knowing that something far worse could happen as the preternatural forces in the dark squared off or simply lashed out at those who had dared to stand against them—mainly Deace and me—I wasn't inclined to go out into the dark and try sniffing around that cave, a cave that even animals stayed away from, in the middle of the night.

It wasn't fear of the dark, not really. Not in the usual sense. I knew better than most people what kind of nightmares were out there. Still, this was more of a tactical matter.

You don't go into enemy territory on the enemy's terms. You go in on your terms. The Otherworld generally dislikes the light of day.

I put the notebook as far away from me as I could get it in the truck bed, shut the tailgate and the cap hatch, and lay down to try to get some sleep, praying that nothing new would blow up before dawn.

Chapter 15

I was pleasantly surprised to wake up and find that the sun was right below the horizon, with no monsters trying to tear my truck apart along with me in it. I kicked the tailgate open, crawled out, washed my face in the river, and then started morning prayers.

There was a lot to get done before that sun went down again.

No sign of Deace, or any sign that anything weird had even happened at all, for that matter. I put the prayer book away and looked at the sky. There were a few high cirrus clouds, but nothing to echo the violent storm that had wracked the valley not that long before.

It didn't make me relax. The tension crackled in the air, at least to me. Maybe it was just my perception, but this was the calm before the storm.

Packing up, making sure my weapons were ready and my holy water flask was full, I started toward the Collins place.

***

I wasn't going to follow Riddle's footsteps and go sneaking around. I drove up to the farmhouse, left the Winchester in the cab as I got out, and walked up the dusty driveway to the front porch.

The house was older, probably built in the '50s. The siding was a little warped, and the paint was peeling in places, though it had the look of a more benign neglect, the kind that came when there was too much work to do to worry too much about keeping up appearances. This was definitely a working farm, as the wear and tear on the trucks and tractors showed. A young man was wrenching on one of those tractors as I walked up. He kept at what he was doing as I approached, apparently oblivious to my presence.

"Morning." I didn't want to startle him, but there wasn't time to mess around. The clock was ticking, even though the preternatural things in the dark don't necessarily follow time the same way we do.

He looked up, seemingly unbothered. "Mornin'." He straightened, wiping his hands on an oily rag. "You're that fella been going around with Sheriff Deace the last few days?"

I raised an eyebrow. "You seem pretty well informed."

He grinned, revealing a missing tooth. "Word gets around quick, especially after the kind of stuff been going on here lately." He sobered, looking over his shoulder. "What brings you here?"

"I heard about a draw on your farm." I could already tell I was getting somewhere when his face went blank. This kid was a good old boy, and he wasn't going to readily admit to being scared, but he knew what draw I was talking about, and he didn't want to have anything to do with it. "One that's completely fenced off, with no access."

"What do you want in there?" He put the rag down on the step leading up into the tractor's cab. "It's dangerous. Sheer drop, loose rocks. Something's off about that area, too. Animals won't go near it."

"That's exactly why I'm interested in it." *Interested* might not have been quite the right word, but it would work.

I squinted toward town, just visible over the rise to the south. "How much of the weirdness made it out here?"

He swallowed. "Enough. Nothing like what I heard about in town, though. Some weird noises and things running through the storm."

From the way he said that, I got a hunch. "You've seen some weird stuff around here before."

He looked away. "We try not to notice it."

That was an old, old way of handling this sort of thing, and it's not a bad way. A lot of folks back in the hollers of Appalachia live the same way. Sometimes the spooks and monsters are just looking for an opening. They're legalistic, and if you break the "rules" then they'll take full advantage. Don't ask about the tortuous mental gymnastics you'd have to go through. Just try to pay them no attention, unless it gets nasty, in which case prayer is your best bet.

Or somebody like me shows up.

"Well, I don't really have that luxury." I nodded toward the lower ground where I suspected the draw was. "Figured I needed to ask before I went poking around there, though."

"You think that draw's got something to do with the weird stuff?" The kid was nervous, as hard as he was trying not to show it.

"Pretty sure." I grimaced. "Not to panic anybody, but I'm pretty sure it's right at the heart of everything going on around here."

He actually paled at that, which was a good trick for a guy as burned brown as he was. "Anything we should do?"

"I'd go inside, lock the doors, and pray, if I were you." I started back toward my truck and the Winchester inside. "I know there's work to get done, but it ain't gonna get done if this goes sideways."

***

After the descriptions in Riddle's notebook, I half expected the area around the draw to be barren rock and dust, with maybe some twisted, thorny, half-dead plants clinging to the ashy soil. Instead, it just looked like the rest of the wilder land around Leutenburg. Bunchgrass and sagebrush, mostly.

The absence of animal life wasn't even all that noticeable right away. This was high prairie or high desert, and aside from birds, you usually didn't see much wildlife, anyway.

When I looked down, though, I could see the hoofprints of cattle in the dusty soil beneath the bunchgrass. And I could see with equal clarity where they stopped and turned away.

The perimeter seemed to be about a hundred yards from the fence. From where I stood, the fence just seemed to be a corral or something, in the middle of open, rolling fields. Only as I got closer could I see the draw itself, the ground falling away from a rocky lip.

Everything had gone quiet as I'd crossed the invisible line that the animals refused to go near. I hadn't really noticed it at first, but now it seemed as if there wasn't even a breath of wind, let alone a birdsong or the stirring of a sage rat in the brush. It was dead silent.

A silence born of fear and death.

It took a long time to reach that rail fence. Not because it was a particularly long distance, but because I paused at every footstep to look and listen. The atmosphere of that place was oppressive, and the closer I got, the worse it became. It was like I was struggling to put my foot down with each step, like I was pushing against an invisible wall, though one that could be no more felt than seen.

Getting over the fence took far more effort than it should have. I wondered if my quarry was in that cave right now. It might explain why I was feeling so much fatigue, while my heart was simultaneously hammering like it was trying to burst out of my chest. I could feel eyes on me.

Dust rose from under my boots as I hit the ground again. The tension seemed to get worse, even as the temperature dropped. I felt the wind again, though it wasn't the gentle breeze that had been rustling the grass before I'd crossed onto the cursed ground. It was a cold, icy blast that plucked at my shirt and stank of blood and death.

I paused, listening. There was a malevolence in this place, and it seemed almost as if it got worse the deeper I went. I was onto something.

Riddle had been, too, and I needed to move fast, preferably without getting my head ripped off or my heart torn out. I didn't think Riddle was going to stay put for long, not if he had the supernatural allies he thought he had.

And it wasn't that shadowman I was worried about.

I worked my way down toward the low ground where the mouth of the draw was a little shallower, allowing for better footing and easier access to the darkened coulee. Easier access and easier retreat, if it came to it.

I'd loaded the Winchester with alternating silver and iron, because I was back to not knowing what I was dealing with. The deeper I got into the unnatural shadow in that little canyon, the more I started to suspect that the holy water in my back pocket was going to get me a lot farther than any of the bullets in my rifle.

The jumble of rocks, dust, and brush down there made for tricky footing, and I had to choose my steps carefully, while still keeping my head up and on a swivel.

The temperature dropped still more, and even as the wind died down, the stench just got worse.

Silence. Nothing stirred down there, and every rock I turned over with my boot, trying to find a solid place to stand, seemed to crash and echo far more loudly than it should have. Maybe that was nerves. There was a distinct feeling that I was treading somewhere I shouldn't be.

Even so, I heard nothing but my own movement as I got deeper into the cleft in the earth, the rocks closing in above my head and the shadow deepening. I could tell I was getting closer to the cave as I moved in, as the rocky walls of the arroyo became blackened with ancient soot along one side.

At least, I kind of assumed it was soot. I probably didn't want to think too hard about the alternatives.

Nothing had jumped out at me as I'd picked my way down the floor of the little coulee, and now I found myself facing the cave, the opening yawning into utter blackness beneath me, my Winchester held ready and my crucifix hanging outside my shirt. It was as silent as the tomb. Nothing stirred. I may as well have been on the surface of the moon.

Except for the lurking sense of a watchful malice, somewhere in that place. It wasn't quite on the level where I could sense that something was *right there*, watching me, but if that thing was really as evil as it seemed to be—nothing else explained the story I'd gotten from Deace—then it wouldn't be acting completely alone. There'd be sorcerous wards, at the very least, on its lair. Possibly worse.

I had to step carefully, or I'd never walk out of this draw, never mind the cave itself.

Something crunched under my boot as I ducked under the low opening, and I looked down, expecting something gruesome, only to find it was a stick. I had to be rattled; I was usually more woods-wise than that. I hadn't broken a branch or a stick on the way in, and I'd barely made a sound getting over the fence.

Holding my breath, despite myself, I froze, listening. No sound, though it seemed to me as if the crunch of the breaking stick echoed down the depths of the cave beneath me.

The tension in the air only intensified. I could *feel* something get more alert.

Maybe my quarry was down there, after all.

I kept working my way in, having to duck my head to keep from scalping myself on the low, stony ceiling. The feeling of a will set against me just got stronger, the deeper I went. Keeping my Winchester at hip height, I found that the rifle got heavier with every step, and the footing seemed to get more treacherous, even though the rocky floor was relatively flat and dry. The descent wasn't even that steep.

I had my light clamped to the rifle's handguard with my off hand. Someday, maybe, I'd figure out a way to mount it, but drilling into the old Winchester to put a light mount, let alone an optic, on it, felt wrong.

The circle of illumination seemed dim and yellow, despite the fact that my light was putting out some serious lumens. I'd seen that happen before. As if I needed any more confirmation that this was a very tainted place.

It was dim enough, though, that I almost missed the body.

I swept the light back as the flash of something that wasn't rock got through my concentration. Sure enough, I'd seen a blood-smeared, pale hand reaching up out of a hole in the rock near the wall of the cave.

Under different circumstances, I might have investigated right away. Instead, I swept my surroundings with light and rifle muzzle again, just to make sure. I didn't want to get drawn toward the obvious bait and then get jumped out of the shadows.

Nothing moved, but despite the oppressive dimness of my light, I was starting to see more as my eyes adjusted. They'd never entirely adjust down there, because that darkness was more than just the absence of light, but my night eyes were getting set enough that I could see that there was more than just rocks along those walls.

Skulls had been carefully arranged around the interior of the cave, set into patterns that made my eyes itch. Many were set with their jaws locked open in what might have been silent screams of agony, terror, or both.

Some still had a bit of flesh and blood on them.

One had more than that.

The slack-jawed, bloodied face staring back at me was obviously dead, though in that place, I couldn't help but feel a sense of foreboding that it was going to suddenly move. I might have a lot of experience with this stuff, but sometimes that only makes it worse.

Neither the hand nor the head moved. There was no sound in the cave except for my breathing and the beating of my heart in my ears. Everything was still.

I moved closer, my finger hovering near the trigger, as much good as that was going to do me if a dead—and dismembered, if I was reading things right—body suddenly came at me. There's no such thing as "undead," not in the way most fantasy and horror movies set it up. But there are spirits and sorceries that can temporarily animate just about anything.

Looking down at the hand, I saw that the body—presumably once belonging to the severed head; they looked like they'd both been dead about the same amount of time—had been smashed into the hole in the rocks, shoved in with bones simply broken when they got in the way. It had taken a terrific amount of force to do that, but that shouldn't surprise me, given what I'd seen so far.

I took a good look at the graying, blood-smeared face staring blindly at me from its niche in the stone wall. I didn't recognize the man, even given the fact that the head was damaged enough to make it pretty difficult even if I'd seen him before. The stump of the neck was ragged, as if the head had been ripped off by main force instead of cut.

That may seem morbidly clinical but trust me, when you're faced with that sort of horror, you get cold and clinical fast, if you don't want to end up running away screaming your head off.

I didn't touch anything. There was a case to be made that this man needed to be properly buried, but not until after this creature was put down, hard.

I said a prayer for the dead man, though I knew nothing about him. I wondered just when this had happened; the corpse was relatively fresh, as if he'd been murdered within the last day. Maybe during the storm?

It looked as if Riddle's conjuring hadn't kept the predator away. It had gotten into town, killed its prey, and gotten out.

The question was, where was it now?

I turned toward the deeper part of the cave and resumed my advance, still scanning and sweeping the darkness with my increasingly anemic light, praying all the way. I'll admit; I was scared. I'd be nuts not to be, going into that thing's lair by myself, in the dark. But unless I found out more about what it was and what it was capable of, I didn't want to risk Deace or any of his fellows down there.

The floor was getting steeper, and there were more rocks ready to roll under my feet. There were also a lot more skulls lining the walls, grinning hollowly at me as my light swept across them. It was all fitting the description in Riddle's notes.

What hadn't been in the notes was the pit that suddenly yawned in front of me, where the floor fell away completely.

It was pitch dark down there, and even as I cast my light down into the blackness, it showed me the sheer stone sides of the pit, and not much else.

Not much except for the old, wooden ladder that had clearly been newly smashed and thrown down to lie broken against the wall, a good ten feet below. Pale, fresh wood glared at me in the dim glow of my light.

Had the creature done that after Riddle came calling? Or had Riddle himself done it, in that coded passage, to keep anyone else from following him down?

That told me something. He'd found a key down there, something that he thought would either let him defeat the predator or gain some control over it. As much as he might protest that he had good intentions in messing around with sorcery, I didn't especially believe it.

Unfortunately, without climbing gear or a ladder, I couldn't go down after him. Which meant he'd bought himself—and the creature we were both hunting—some time.

The hackles standing straight up on the back of my neck at the thought of turning my back on that yawning chasm, I turned and headed back up toward the daylight.

I'd have to move quickly. Especially if the predator wasn't in the cave.

Where was it, and what was it doing while I was down here?

Chapter 16

To my surprise, I made it out into the daylight without incident. I still felt like I was being watched, and as I picked my way back along the floor of the coulee, I could have sworn I saw shadows move a couple of times. Something had changed while I'd been down there in the dark, but I still couldn't quite put my finger on just what it was.

To some extent, I didn't need to. The thunderstorm tension in the air had redoubled. While I might not have seen anything but skulls and the recently dead down there, I'd definitely disturbed something.

Maybe the predator just didn't want to come at a Witch Hunter head to head. Or maybe it did have sentinels, and now they were stalking me.

Either way, things were moving. That had become inevitable after that sorcerous storm. The clock was ticking.

I was almost back to the fence when something made me stop. I spun around, the rifle in my shoulder, looking across the sagebrush and bunchgrass. This time I was sure I saw something dark flatten itself to the ground and slither away.

Watching where it had disappeared, I could tell that it wasn't gone. It was still lurking there, flattened down to the ground to a degree impossible for a human being, still watching me. I just didn't know where, and I couldn't be sure that it hadn't slipped somewhere else as soon as it had gotten out of my line of sight.

I thought about calling out to it, daring it to come after me. That really wasn't a good idea, and I wondered if it was trying to push that thought into my head. Directly bandying words with these things is usually a trap.

When I started to turn away, though, I caught its movement out of the corner of my eye. Gritting my teeth, I turned back toward it. I couldn't turn my back on this thing. It was stalking me, and regardless, it was a threat.

I held my ground, my eyes moving over the brush. Unfortunately, I knew that it probably wasn't going to come straight at me. That wasn't the way these creatures worked. They'd come at you from the side, from behind, while trying to draw your attention away.

Fortunately, I had some experience with these sorts of critters.

I waited, rifle partly leveled, watching and listening. The silence was still there, just as it had been since I'd crossed that invisible line that the animals wouldn't go near, but sound wasn't the only indicator.

The thing about the Otherworld is that it doesn't operate by the same rules as the waking world under the sun. It still has rules, though, and while they tend to seem obscure and arbitrary, you can figure them out after a while.

In this case, I was pretty sure I knew what I was up against, and so I stayed still until the last possible moment, then turned around suddenly.

The creature looked like a giant snake, but it was made of smoke and shadow. It recoiled as I faced it, but I locked gazes with it. Not many Otherworlders are the type you want to make eye contact with, but something had told me that this thing was trying too hard to be sneaky.

It froze as I stared it down, though after a second I realized that it wasn't quite looking me in the eye. Its eyes were fixed on my chest, where my silver crucifix was hanging from its leather thong. It wanted to retreat, but it was frozen in place.

Those eyes, the only solid-looking part of the creature, looked up. They were yellow and watery, which seemed strange in a thing seemingly made from smoke and shadow.

Then, with a hiss, it was gone.

I bit back a curse. I'd gotten sloppy, hoping in my haste that my timing and the sight of the crucifix might have surprised it. I should have known better. Something as old and dangerous as our predator wouldn't have pushovers as its sentinels.

Scanning my surroundings, I felt the temperature, which had started to rise as I'd gotten closer to that invisible line, begin to drop again. The ground started to look dim and blurry, and the sun overhead seemed muted, as if a pall of smoke had passed in front of it.

"Oh, crap." This thing was a lot worse than I'd thought. Some low-level glorified trickster wasn't going to be able to have that kind of sway over the environment.

"*Yes.*" The voice seemed to come from the rattling of sagebrush in the wind that had suddenly picked up, even though it didn't stir the murk that was settling over the ground. It didn't say anything more. It didn't need to. It was simply confirming my assessment, that this was very, very bad.

I'd dealt with very, very bad before, but this was hardly the time. This thing was trying to stop me or delay me before I could interfere with its master.

How I knew it wasn't my quarry, I really couldn't say. I just did. This shadow-serpent was effectively a hired gun, nothing more.

That didn't make it any less dangerous. It just made it an obstacle I couldn't afford. Nor could anyone back in Leutenburg.

Something dark slithered through the brush off to my right, and even as I pivoted toward it, I realized it was a decoy. I spun back to the right, getting a single shot off at the dark snake as it reared up to strike, but it faded away as my bullet went right through the middle of its head. A hiss that might have been laughter susurrated through the brush.

It hit me then, and I hadn't even seen it coming. It came out of the brush off to the right, where I'd first seen the movement, and I went sprawling, almost losing my grip on the Winchester as I fell into a patch of sagebrush. Apparently, there was some prickly pear in there, too, judging by the spines that went into my shoulder.

I rolled out of the way, scrambling to my feet, but it was gone. I gritted my teeth as I stayed on a knee, my rifle over my thigh. It could have had me, unless someone was really looking out for me. That had happened before, but I didn't think it was the case this time.

This thing was toying with me. Like a cat playing with a mouse.

It wasn't necessary for its delaying tactics. It was just being cruel, as many of these things can be.

I caught it this time, and even as it reversed the maneuver, I was ready for it. It ducked away as my rifle came level, but the hiss that rattled through the brush was angrier than before.

I needed to get away and deal with this thing later. The longer it kept me here, the more time Riddle, his own master—though he'd probably call whatever dark spirit it was a "sponsor" or something—and the predator had to get up to whatever evil they were after. If I was stuck here…

Working my way a few more steps toward the line, I got hit again. I was ready for it, though it still managed to get my eyes and muzzle looking in the wrong direction. I rolled aside as it hit, and it slithered into the brush, leaving behind a deadly cold on my leg. It was so bad that I almost fell, and I could barely walk for the next few steps.

But I was a little closer. And I wasn't out of tools in the toolbox.

Holy water is a potent weapon against the Abyss and its allies in the Otherworld. Its counterpart is blessed salt. And I just happened to have some in my pocket.

Holy water harkens back to baptism, but the salt symbolizes the faith itself. So, against some of the weirder and more ambivalent Otherworlders, it's sometimes hit or miss. I had nothing to lose by trying, though.

So, as I scrambled back, limping on a leg gone numb, hoping that there wasn't some Otherworldly poison coursing through my veins, I pulled the little container out of my pocket, hopefully disguising the movement with my rifle and my limp, and poured a small line of the salt on the ground between me and where that thing had disappeared.

"Playing hard to get, huh?" At that point, I didn't see much point in *not* antagonizing it. It was already coming at me. I may as well draw it out, especially since I now had—potentially—a trap set for it. "Must be hard, doing some more powerful creature's bidding, and then not even being tough enough to finish the job."

"*I have all the time I need. I shall feast on your fear before I drink your blood, as you spasm out your last breaths while my venom burns your veins.*"

It was getting cocky, which was good. I spilled more blessed salt on the ground, not without a silent prayer that, through the virtue invested in it by the blessing, I might gain a few more minutes to live.

If it was banished by contact with the exorcised salt, so much the better.

It came at me again, once again feinting to one side, then coming from the other. Except they were both feints, I realized, as I snapped my rifle toward the second shadow only to have it disappear in a writhing cloud of smoke.

It was too late for the shadow serpent, though.

While its mirror image dissolved, it suddenly came up out of the brush, just behind me and to my right, almost directly between me and the draw. It struck at me from there, and while it was right at the end of my line of salt, it wasn't quite all the way around it.

There was a flare that might have been flame, and the thing suddenly reared back, twisting and writhing as sparks flew from its flank. Its hiss was equal parts rage and pain.

I shot it then, no longer sure whether I had iron or silver chambered. The bullet smacked into it with surprising solidity, sending it flopping backward, though it didn't seem to do much more than that.

Juggling rifle and salt container, I backed up some more, hardly daring to take my eyes off that thing. Levering another round into the chamber, I shot it again.

That round did some more, though it still just seemed like I'd punched it really hard. The bullet didn't seem to penetrate or do much damage. I realized I'd spilled the rest of the salt anyway, so I dropped the container and got a better grip on the rifle.

"I don't have time for your crap." I shot it again. Even less effect, but the contact with the salt had really messed it up. It was still twisting and thrashing in agony on the ground, more sparks flying off the livid scar on its side, though fortunately, they weren't setting the grass and brush ablaze. "You've got a choice. You can crawl back into whatever pit you slithered out of, or I can send you there the hard way." There was some bluster in my words, since I didn't know for sure how I'd accomplish that, especially as I levered another silver-tipped bullet into the chamber and shot it in the head, accomplishing not much more than beating it up some more.

It was clearly evil enough that contact with holy things was painful, but I wasn't an exorcist, and I was out of salt.

I did have holy water, though.

It was still thrashing on the ground, but it had craned its neck to glare at me, fangs glinting in the darkness of its maw. They looked metal, somehow, but I was beginning to realize that I probably shouldn't take anything about this creature's appearance at face value. After all, it had used illusion and misdirection a lot already.

I set my rifle on my shoulder and drew out the flask of holy water, unscrewing the cap with one hand. I lifted it as I stepped over the wounded monster, and I saw a mix of utter hatred and abject terror in those eyes.

Then, suddenly, it vanished. A black cloud seemed to race away over the ground, and the twisted, smoking, rotting remains of a rattlesnake twitched and died in the dust at my feet.

I felt a chill that had nothing to do with the ambient temperature. That had been bad, bad medicine. It might have been small fry, but that dark shadow that had been using the snake as its anchor had come right out of the Abyss.

As I thumbed more cartridges into my Winchester and turned back toward the farm and my truck, I realized that, even though the thing animating the snake was gone, the sun was as anemic and wan as it had been before.

Meaning that I really wasn't out of the woods yet. The shadow-serpent had kept me occupied for long enough that things were happening, and a pall of what looked like yellowish smoke hung over Leutenburg.

I broke into a run.

Chapter 17

The kid who'd been working on the tractor had been on the alert, a rifle in his hands, as I came up from the draw. He didn't quite point it at me as I approached, but he was clearly wary. He had to have heard my shots, and from the look on his face, that draw was spooky enough that he really wasn't sure if I was me, or something trying to look like me.

While I wasn't sure just how well it would work, I held up the silver crucifix. "I'm not one of the monsters."

For a moment, he didn't react. He didn't lower the gun, but he didn't blast me, either. My own rifle was well off line, and I wasn't sure that I could snap it up fast enough if he did try to shoot me. I really didn't want to get in a firefight with a local farmer, but I didn't intend to get my head blown off, either.

Finally, he relaxed. "Wasn't sure what to think, hearing all the commotion down there." He nodded in the direction of town. "And there's that."

I followed his gaze. I'd been focused enough on getting back to my truck that I hadn't been keeping track of the pall over Leutenburg. It had grown, towering high above the town, flattening out in an anvil head that looked like a thunderstorm had touched down on the ground, except that it was a dull, poisonous yellow. There was nothing natural about that smoke pall.

It was different from the storm, but all that meant was that either Riddle had tried something new, or the predator I was hunting had decided to fully step onto the field.

With a heavy sigh, I climbed into my truck and got on the road, heading back into town, driving toward that sickly cloud of unnatural haze.

***

It wasn't the first time I'd gone into a town under preternatural assault. I'd gone through a town where it was raining blood one night. Fortunately, I'd been alongside The Captain at the time, and as terrifying as that was, given that he's a being capable of unmaking worlds, there's not much in this universe that can touch him.

That had been a terrible night, the darkness full of monsters and horrors, the screams and howls echoing through the blood-soaked gloom.

This was different.

Everything got quiet as I passed inside the sickly yellow cloud. Even the rumble of my truck's engine got muted. The buildings and trees were dim, diffuse silhouettes, even though they were only a few yards away. The light never quite went away, but everything turned to a murky, brown twilight as I drove deeper into town.

About half a mile in, I almost collided with a van in the middle of the road, stomping on the brakes at the last moment and bringing my truck to a halt inches from the rear bumper. The van was slewed partway toward the sidewalk, the doors open, with no movement anywhere near it.

I parked my truck, hoping and praying it would stay intact if I left it, and got out. Visibility was too bad to try to drive much farther in this muck.

As soon as I opened my door, I smelled sulfur. That was bad. Not that there was anything good in this situation at all.

I stepped away from my truck, examining the van in front of me. The engine was off and there was no sign of anyone in or around it. At least, not until I stepped closer, and saw a form crumpled on the street not far from the driver's door.

Keeping my eyes up, I advanced on the shape of the fallen body, finding a woman lying face down on the pavement. She was breathing, but she wasn't moving. I couldn't find any wounds, so I let her be.

As I straightened, I got a sudden sense that I was being watched, closely. I scanned the street, but I could barely see the shapes of the buildings, let alone through the windows. There was no sound.

Or was there? I held my breath, listening. Were there whispers in the haze? Movement, just out of sight? I turned quickly, looking for a source for the strange noises I might have only imagined, but only stillness met my eyes and my leveled Winchester muzzle.

The whispers were there, but it was hard to make out if they were there in my ears, or just in my head. Something about that yellow-brown cloud, that just *looked* toxic, though so far, aside from the stench, I wasn't choking or coughing or anything.

Something was happening, but at least from here, it seemed to be entirely silent. Either there was some serious sorcery at work here, or else the opposing monsters were stalking each other in the gloom and hadn't actually come to grips yet.

I wasn't sure which alternative was worse.

Moving toward the sidewalk, I kept scanning, praying silently as I went, hoping that this wasn't the time I was about to get my head ripped off by something I hadn't seen until it was too late. I needed to move, though. I couldn't afford to freeze in the murk, peering through the haze and wondering what was happening.

Events had already gotten ahead of me, and so I needed to find out where I was and then decide where to go next.

The storefront loomed in front of me as I stepped onto the sidewalk. It was the same place where I'd first paused on the way into town, wondering why I felt so unsettled on the streets of Leutenburg.

That was ominous.

Not that superstition had any place in my profession. But even so, things rarely happen by accident, and even the darkness can give a man nudges. When they did that, it usually wasn't for the target's benefit.

Whispers again. I turned slowly, paying more attention to my peripheral vision than what was right in front of me. The Otherworld tends to like to sneak around just out of sight, so if you're going to spot something, it's probably going to be that way.

Nothing. No movement. No shadows where there shouldn't be any—though in the dim light in that cloud of preternatural smog it was hard to say where the shadows shouldn't be. The sense of being watched was getting even more intense, though.

At least I knew where I was. I hadn't been in town quite long enough to have a full map in my head, but Leutenburg wasn't that big, and I had developed a habit over time of taking in as much detail about my surroundings as possible.

I thought over where the next step might be. Where was the epicenter of this disaster?

The sheriff's office. That was where Riddle was, and if Riddle was playing the game that I suspected he was, then this was probably centered around him, somehow. Either he was causing it...

Or the predator had decided that here was the reckoning.

As I started to work my way down the street, it occurred to me that there was a third possibility. If the shadowman had truly taken offense at Riddle's attempts, then it might be involved as well. I doubted it, unless it had really been better at lying to a Witch Hunter than I'd thought, but it was still a possibility.

Turned out, it was involved, just not the way I thought.

"*Witch Hunter.*" The voice seemed to come from everywhere and nowhere at once. "*You should go back. My quarrel is not with you.*"

I looked up. I knew the voice, even though I couldn't see anything. I'd heard it not that long ago. "I don't care. Stay out of my way, Shadowman. Go do your penance and stay in the shadows, or I'll have to deal with you like the other shadowman in Silverton." I didn't know if this one might know about that incident, but it was likely. The Otherworld made the Lance Corporal Underground in the Marine Corps look amateur.

There might have been a snarl in the murk, but it was different from what might be a threat. It was a sound of frustration and, almost, agony. As if it was a real wrench for the Otherworlder to turn aside from its vendetta. It probably was. Even if this shadowman was telling the truth, that he was on a quest of penance until the end times, that

Otherworld pride ran deep, deeper than any merely human arrogance.

I took another step, waiting for the explosion. If the shadowman decided to fight, instead of give up his vengeance—presumably on Riddle—then this was going to get really interesting, really fast.

"*I cannot stand against you, Witch Hunter.*" There was a mix of resignation and anger in the words. "*Beware. Trust not your eyes.*"

There was a strange sense of emptiness and silence a second later. Even without seeing the dark figure, I could tell that the shadowman was gone. It might be a grudging surrender, but it had bowed out when I'd told it to.

That was a good sign, though I still had to worry about Riddle and the Leutenburg Killer, whatever it was.

I was two more blocks from the sheriff's office, judging by my memory of the area. I paused for a second to get my bearings. I didn't want to get turned around, and I was sure that part of the reason for the unnatural haze cloaking Leutenburg was to make sure that anyone who was still conscious did get turned around and vulnerable.

Whether Riddle or the Killer had conjured it, I didn't know. Under some circumstances, it might not matter, but here, it really did.

Moving carefully and slowly, still whispering a litany under my breath, I started up the street, staying close to the buildings but pieing off every opening as I passed it. Again, more out of habit than actual utility against the Otherworld or the Abyss, but better to be doing something than just tooling along, waiting to get jumped.

Step by step, I pushed through the whispers, watching the shadows and the vague movement at the corners of my eyes. The haze seemed to be alive, though every time I turned toward the movement or the shadows, what I thought I'd seen faded quickly.

The quiet was the most unnerving part, though. I was increasingly convinced that most of the movement was illusion, intended to sow terror. The whispers were the same.

It was the fact that everything else was so quiet that was disturbing. None of the howls or screeches of the previous night echoed through the smog. It was as if there was some massive game of cat-and-mouse afoot, and while it was probable that it was mostly between Riddle and the Killer, I couldn't help feeling like I was the mouse.

Still, I reached the next intersection without getting attacked. Easing my eye around the corner, I scanned the street that led toward city hall and the county courthouse.

Nothing. Stillness, except for the writhing tendrils of murk twisting between the cars on the street. No one was out on the street, at least no one who was moving. I thought I saw another body sprawled on the street beneath an open car door.

That made me narrow my eyes as I kept scanning, the litany unpaused. Why was I unaffected by this strange, soporific fog?

I didn't stick around wondering for too long. Whether it was a trap, or my guardian angel was hard at work, the fact remained that the things that went bump in the night were afoot, and so was I.

The courthouse, which contained the sheriff's office, was little more than a vague, blocky shadow in the murk from where I stood. I was going to have to get closer. Checking my six one more time, I started in.

The stench of sulfur got worse as I moved toward the courthouse, and I started to hear noises over the faint susurration of the ceaseless whispers. They still weren't the bone-chilling howls and cries that had echoed around the old Dermody place, but a ceaseless, frantic scratching, like fingernails on wood, but far louder. As if hundreds of creatures were trying to claw their way inside the courthouse.

I couldn't see any of them as I got closer, but I could see the marks on the doors. Something was attacking the entrance to the courthouse. I just couldn't see it.

Then the doors shuddered, though not as if something was trying to get in. Instead, it looked almost like something was trying to get *out*.

Something dark settled on top of the courthouse, but when I swiveled eyes and muzzle up toward it, it floated away.

It looked to me as if neither party clashing here really wanted to tangle with me *and* each other, and neither one trusted the other enough to gang up on me. That was interesting.

I felt eyes on me, and turned to search the street, between the parked trucks and a couple of cars stopped in the middle of the road.

The figure standing there seemed cloaked in the haze, almost as if it had drawn the murk around itself, but I could still see it, dim though it might be. I squinted, and locked eyes with the same face that I'd seen, bloody and disembodied, in the cave.

The chill that ran down my spine didn't slow me down. I'd been through a bit too much of this stuff to freeze when I was confronted with the seemingly impossible. I snapped my Winchester toward the sneering face, but then it was gone, almost as quickly as I had spotted it. That thing moved *fast*.

"*Clever.*" The voice seemed to reverberate in much the same way the shadowman's had, though it sounded decidedly different. Still deep, there was a sneering bite to it that was in decided contrast to the shadowman's tone. "*So, you have been trespassing and snooping, have you? How else would you have recognized me?*" The voice was changing direction quickly as the creature moved, though at least it wasn't suddenly coming from opposite sides of the street. It was moving fast, somehow staying out of sight, but it wasn't teleporting or anything.

It was moving fast enough that it was hard to track it by sound, but it was all I had. I still overshot as it appeared next to one of the cars sitting in the middle of the street, that had stopped halfway across the line as the driver had apparently managed to stomp on the brake just before passing out.

I'll admit it. I hesitated. It wasn't the decapitated man's face that was looking back at me now, though the figure standing there was still cloaked in wisps of yellow smog. I didn't recognize the bearded man at all, and I would have dismissed him as a mere bystander, who had somehow escaped getting knocked unconscious by the yellow haze, if I hadn't looked in his eyes.

While they looked like human eyes, there was something about them that was just wrong. I couldn't say what it was, except that there was something simultaneously soulless and dead, as well as lit with an insane, bloodthirsty glee.

I'd seen just enough of the Killer's eyes a few seconds before to know that I was looking at the same creature. One that could change its shape from moment to moment.

Great.

I whipped my rifle into my shoulder, though it was already blurring into motion again. *"You really shouldn't be getting between me and my prey. Granted, I wouldn't have let you live, anyway. Interfering holy busybodies like you just can't leave well enough alone. It's probably just as well that you're here, now, though you're complicating things more than I'd like. Still, at least I won't have to chase you down."*

"You're not chasing squat, blood-sucker." I didn't know or care whether that was the way this thing really killed. I just wanted to get under its skin. "You're not tangling with some wandering preacher man."

It didn't answer, which was just as well. I spared a glance up at the courthouse, wondering what kind of nightmare was going on in there with Riddle presumably throwing his sorcery around, but I had my hands full with the shapeshifting killer.

Catching a glimpse of movement swirling through the haze, I swung my rifle to track it. As fast as it was moving, I was only going to get a split second to take a shot, especially since I was in the middle of town and didn't want to miss and hit anyone on the other side.

It stopped almost on the opposite end of the street, coming out of a swirl of smog with yet another face, this one that of a small, attractive blonde. It batted its insane eyes at me, shoving its lower lip out in a pout. *"You wouldn't shoot this pretty little thing, would you?"* It was advancing on me, hips swaying, as if it meant to seduce me somehow. It was trying to close the distance so it could get its claws on me.

"Does that really work?" I asked, just before I blew a hole through its chest.

It was a gamble, more than my comment might have suggested. I still had the alternating iron and silver rounds, since I really didn't know which was going to work on this thing, if either.

Apparently, the iron didn't do much.

It stopped dead, rocked back on its heels, but then it looked down at the suspiciously bloodless hole in its chest, then back up at me, its features rippling. It opened its mouth in a snarl, taking a breath to say something, when I shot it again, this time right through the teeth.

The heavy round with the silver ball embedded in its hollow nose smashed right through the skull, spattering bits of bone, brain, and hair—though, again, almost no blood—across the window of the vehicle parked just behind the thing. It stopped again, those eyes still glaring at me with their insane hatred, but it rocked back on its heels and then crumpled to the ground.

The sickly yellow cloud didn't disperse, like I'd halfway expected it to. It still clung to the town, cloaking everything in a leprous fog, filling my nostrils with that noxious stink, which now that I had a second to breathe, struck me as a little more metallic than just the smell of sulfur.

I levered another round into the Winchester's chamber, but I didn't shoot the thing again, as tempting as that might have been. Something was still very off here, especially the lack of blood. I half expected it to pull its head together and start to rise off the ground, but it still lay there, motionless, its blank, dead eyes—now a featureless black—staring sightlessly at the sky.

While shooting it again might be counterproductive, I wasn't going to just assume that it was dead and turn my back on it without taking some precautions.

Pulling the holy water flask out of my back pocket, I splashed some of it on the corpse in a vague sign of the cross.

Nothing happened; no smoking, screaming, or bursting into flames. If it was playing possum, it was doing a pretty good job of it, better than any Otherworlder or thing of the Abyss I'd ever run across.

Still, as I looked down at it, though it hadn't changed shape, I couldn't help but suspect that this wasn't over yet.

And it wasn't. The doors to the courthouse blew open a moment later.

I pivoted around, bringing the Winchester back up, even though it meant letting the holy water flask fall to the street. I didn't have a chance to bring it to bear, though, before a wall of black smoke slammed into me and *threw* me into the truck parked on the side of the road. I hit hard enough that I saw stars, the wind instantly knocked out of me. I lost my grip on the Winchester, and it fell to the pavement with a clatter, scarring up the already battered bluing and putting yet another ding in the old walnut stock.

Falling to all fours, wracked with pain, I gasped for air, sucking hard and coughing, as I looked up to see Riddle coming out of the courthouse.

He wasn't walking. Nor was he running. He was *floating*, levitating as he glided down the handful of courthouse steps toward the street.

That tore it. Riddle wasn't some foolish dabbler in over his head. He was a *practitioner*.

Which told me why the murk hadn't dispersed as soon as I'd put the Killer down. And made this entire situation far more dangerous than it had been just with a supernatural, apparently immortal predator stalking the town.

He lifted his hands, and another wave of that black smoke swept out and slammed into me, knocking me back into the vehicle again. I was a bit more ready for it this time, and as I whispered the Holy Name, it dampened the impact, though it still hurt.

"I'm not sure whether to thank you or curse you, Mr. Horn." He wasn't advancing on me, but heading down the street, away from the courthouse. "You've caused me an untold amount of trouble, bringing eyes on my activities that I would rather remain blind, interfering with my work. On the other hand, you just advanced my plan considerably without my having to risk myself any further." He looked down at the stiffened corpse of the chameleon on the ground near me. When he looked up at me, there was about as much humanity in his stare as there had been in the Killer's eyes.

"Now, only because you did help, despite your do-gooder interference, I'll do you a favor. Stay down and I won't kill you. You're done here. Go crawl back into your church and pray." He laughed. "Maybe it will give you some comfort."

Another wave of black, oily smoke smacked me sideways, sending me tumbling away from my rifle. My pistol dug painfully into my side as I rolled to a stop with a groan.

I was still trying to get some air into my lungs. For a long moment, as he vanished down the street, I simply couldn't do anything but lie there, hurt, and gasp for air.

I rolled onto my back, getting off my pistol and staring at the sky as I gulped breaths into slowly recovering lungs. *That didn't go according to plan.*

Finally, though I was far from fully recovered, I rolled back over and levered myself to my knees, then rose unsteadily to my feet. My entire body felt like one enormous bruise, my throat hurt from trying to regain my wind, and I was pretty sure I was bleeding in a couple of places. I staggered over to my Winchester and dragged it up off the ground, making sure it was still in working order. That antique weapon had been through a lot, but it still kept ticking.

Straightening against the aches, I looked around. The yellow mist was finally dispersing, its purpose done. No one on the street was moving, and when I glanced up toward the courthouse, I couldn't help but wince. I could only imagine how bad it had been in there, and I hoped and prayed that Deace and his people were all right.

I crossed myself, said a quick prayer for their safety, and then turned around and headed back toward my truck.

I thought I knew where Riddle was going, and if I couldn't beat him there, maybe I could corner him, at least.

I didn't know why he was doing what he was doing, but it was apparent that the Leutenburg Killer had had something he wanted. Which meant I was going to have to take it away from him.

Lucky me.

Chapter 18

Fortunately, my truck started up. After the weirdness of that sorcerous cloud, I wasn't so sure that it would. Sorcery can muck up technology pretty bad, and this truck was a lot fancier and more complicated than my old F100.

I backed up and steered around the stopped minivan and the body of the woman in the street. I suspected that most of the folks in Leutenburg were going to need medical attention soon, but I wasn't a doctor, and I had other responsibilities at the moment.

The streets were an obstacle course, at least around downtown. It had been the busy part of the day, with people going to work, at least those who worked in town instead of the farms around the outside. There were cars either just stopped or outright wrecked all along the street, and I had to weave through them to get out of town.

Fortunately, Leutenburg being a small town worked to my advantage, and I was out of town quicker than Riddle might have liked. He was still well ahead of me, though, and I put the pedal to the metal to catch up. I wasn't too worried about getting pulled over; Deace and his boys had more pressing things on their minds at the moment.

***

I half expected the Collins farm to be wreathed in the same poisonous yellow fog that had put Leutenburg into a nightmare-wracked slumber, but everything seemed normal.

Clouds had moved in, but when I glanced up at them, they looked like regular, ordinary clouds. There was weather coming in, but it didn't look to me like Riddle had anything to do with it.

The farmhouse was still and dark, no lights on even as the clouds turned the afternoon into twilight. That might not have been all that strange, if everyone was out working, but there was no sign of anyone in the fields nearby, either.

Parking on the road, I stepped out, making sure the Winchester was topped off and that I didn't have any empty loops on my belt. I wasn't necessarily expecting a firefight, but if Riddle had beaten me here—and I had no reason to believe he hadn't—then there could be a lot of nasty surprises waiting for me between here and the Killer's hole.

It was strangely quiet as I moved toward the house. So quiet that the crunch of gravel under my boots sounded deafeningly loud. I couldn't hear or feel any wind, which was strange with the cloud cover, and no birds or insects were sounding their calls or buzzings. It was an unnatural silence, and the sort of quiet that made someone in my line of work take some pause. It meant that there were Otherworldly forces at work.

Not that that was a surprise at that point.

I stepped up on the porch, passing the tractor that the younger man had been working on the last time I'd been there. There were no tools out or any other sign that he'd suddenly left it behind, but there was still something off here.

No kidding.

I knocked on the door, and it swung open slightly under my knuckles. That wasn't good, though I couldn't say I was entirely surprised, given what I'd seen and heard so far.

"Anyone here?" It might seem like a dumb stunt from a horror movie, where the characters do some of the stupidest things imaginable just to set them up for the jump scare, but I couldn't just go barging into someone's house just because the door wasn't latched. I had to announce my presence, kind of like a cop, and see if anyone answered, or if I heard or saw anything that might give me a reason to go in. I might suspect something was amiss, but that wasn't enough.

Even as shadowy a world as I worked in, there were still rules.

I heard something, a faint scratching and what might have been an equally faint moan of pain or fear. It was enough. I shoved the door the rest of the way open with my rifle muzzle, scanning the dark inside as I went.

The stench hit my nostrils as soon as I crossed the threshold, and I knew that I hadn't made a mistake coming in here. Riddle—or something—had targeted the Collins place, probably to make sure no one interfered with whatever he was doing here.

The young man I'd spoken to earlier was sitting on the floor just inside, staring at nothing, a rictus of sheer horror on his face. He was alive; I could tell that much by the fact that he was panting and shaking as he sat there, staring without blinking.

I snapped my fingers in front of his face, but there was no sign he was even aware of me. With a grimace, I shook my head and looked around the darkened room. The blinds had been drawn for some reason, which told me that Riddle—or something he'd conjured—had been in here, actively doing things and not just trying to get into the Collins' heads.

"I'll set this right." I didn't know if the young feller could hear me, but if he could, maybe it would give him something to hold onto, something to start bringing him back from the brink. I made the sign of the cross, starting the first deliverance prayer. *I could really use an exorcist here.*

I could use all sorts of things, but sometimes we've just got to work with what we've got. There wasn't time to go running to the diocese for heavy-hitter support.

Moving deeper into the living room, I saw more of how the Collinses lived. They weren't wealthy, but they didn't live in a pigsty, either. The furniture was old and worn, and it looked like they hadn't bought much of anything new in quite a few years, but it was mostly neat—except where things had been flung around the room, apparently during the incursion that had left the younger Collins staring into space and shaking.

The stink got worse the deeper in I got. The living room opened onto the kitchen and the dining room, small as both were, and the floor was littered with smashed dishes and utensils, while the cupboards in the kitchen all hung open, the shelves swept bare. An older woman, her face lined, bags under her eyes, was standing there, her hands on the counter behind her, staring sightlessly at the middle of the living room, shaking almost as bad as the younger man behind me.

I paused, looking down at the floor in front of me, near the center of the living room. There was a sigil burned into the carpet. Not one I recognized, but that didn't say much. It was something out of the Abyss, that was all that I really needed to know.

A low, evil laugh whispered through the room. Looking around, I couldn't see anything, but that shouldn't have been any surprise.

"So predictable. Fooled by your sanctimonious drivel into walking into what is now my *house,* my *domain."* That chuckle sounded positively vile, as if the thing making it was imagining all sorts of depraved monstrosities, and taking great pleasure in them. *"Now he has left you to me."*

The voice was moving as it whispered. It seemed to come from first one corner, then another. Then it seemed to be coming from over by the young man near the front door.

"How shall we proceed? Should I make one of them kill the other, while I make you watch? Or should I make you kill them? Or..." It laughed again, the sound somehow even worse than before. *"Perhaps I will get into their minds, one by one, and make* them *do it to* themselves!"

If I hadn't already had years of experience with these things, that would have been truly appalling. Now, maybe I've just gotten jaded, but the fact of the matter is that most of these creatures are looking for a reaction more than anything else. Not that they're not dangerous, but they are sadists at their core, and they relish all the fear and terror they can bring about.

Of course, they're not really mind readers, no matter how much they might be able to pick out from expressions, words, and actions, far more than you or I could, but they can't be *sure* what you're thinking. Which sometimes leads them to miscalculate.

"You talk pretty big for a glorified goblin that got roped into doing a two-bit sorcerer's bidding." I snorted. "To listen to you, somebody might think that you're some harbinger of doom, when the reality is, you're the speed bump."

That thing might have gloated about people being predictable, but the pride that puts so much of the

Otherworld on the wrong side of the eternal struggle is far more so.

With a shriek, the thing came up out of a crack in the floor, a dark, hazy wraith that quickly coalesced into what looked like a bipedal iguana made of smoke, with red eyes that were points of flame within the hardening cloud.

I might have shot it, but I had a hunch. There were Otherworlders that could squeeze themselves into spaces that would be impossible for ordinary humans or animals, but something about Riddle's sorcery stank of the Abyss. I didn't think this thing was a part of the physical world, as tenuous as the Otherworld's connection could be.

So, I hit it with holy water while beginning a deliverance prayer.

It screamed, the holy water practically splitting it in half as it started to dissolve. I advanced on it, the silver crucifix swinging from its thong around my neck, and the apparition recoiled, even as it seemed to be coming apart.

"Get out!" I made the sign of the cross with the holy water again, and it snaked backward, leaking bits of itself into nothingness, fetching up against the wall and climbing halfway to the ceiling.

"*You can't force me out!*" Demons tend to be legalistic, as I've pointed out, but I figured it would be hard pressed to make the legal argument that it deserved to be there, tormenting the Collinses. Sometimes they could make it stick, though more through a combination of their targets' sinfulness—which generally counts against all of us—and their own stubbornness.

This was a minor spirit, though, and it was already in retreat. "You don't have a right to be here just because some tinpot occultist said you could. And even if you had your hooks in, I've got heavier forces behind me than you do. *Get out!*" I lifted the holy water flask again, and this time the thing vanished, howling out of the window with a gust of wind, dissolving in the wan sunlight outside as it went.

The woman in the kitchen slumped suddenly, blinking as she looked around and started to slide toward the floor. The young man at the doorway started, his head whipping around toward me as he came back from whatever waking nightmare that thing had dragged him into.

I wanted to stay and make sure they were okay. I needed to—or somebody needed to. The truth was that nobody in this town was going to be okay for a while. Father Gascone was going to have a lot on his hands when he came to town for Mass next Sunday.

But this was only going to get worse if I didn't get down into the Killer's hole and stop Riddle. Whatever he was up to.

"You're going to be all right." I tried to be as reassuring as I could be, but I tend to look like a heavily armed vagrant at the best of times, and I didn't think either of them had noticed me entering their house. "It's gone. But right now, I've got to go after the guy who sicced it on you, so that it stays gone."

The woman didn't seem to hear, her hands over her face while she shook and cried. The young man staggered to his feet. He seemed to recognize me from earlier. "I should come with you." The shaking in his hands contrasted with his brave intentions.

I shook my head, already moving toward the door. "Stay here. I can't keep an eye on you and watch for whatever other nasty surprises he's set up, and you're not trained or prepared for this."

He looked pained. "What can we do?"

"Pray."

Chapter 19

The wind was kicking by the time I got back outside. It seemed pretty natural, and I could smell rain in the distance, but that didn't mean Riddle and his dark master weren't helping things along.

No, I wasn't laying all of this just on Riddle. Nobody goes down that route without something dark, nasty, and evil helping them along. Sure, the Devil isn't behind all evil. We're capable of plenty, ourselves. But this kind of sorcery doesn't just happen. *Something* was lending him some power, and from the looks of things, it was something pretty high up—or low down, if you wanted to get all C.S. Lewis—in the hierarchy of the Abyss.

So, you can bet I was praying hard as I closed in on the cut where the Killer had had its hole.

The fence had been smashed, as if by a giant fist. Since Riddle had been levitating the last time I'd seen him, I could only imagine that the destruction had been wrought out of spite more than anything else. I still kept my eyes moving as I stepped over the splinters on the ground, knowing that he'd have left some sort of nasty surprise for me, even if he'd thought that I was lying beaten on the street back in town.

Sure enough, there was just such a surprise waiting.

"Didn't I stab you once?"

The one-eyed hopping little monstrosity didn't speak, though its toothy maw was fixed in a lunatic grin as it bounced out from behind a rock, waving its stone-tipped spear at me. Nor did the half dozen or so other little horrors that appeared behind him.

With only eight rounds in the tube, and half of them likely to be ineffective, this was a situation that required caution and strategy.

I shot the lead gremlin, or whatever it was, in the face, holding my sights on the thing just long enough to make sure it went down as I levered the next round into the chamber. My next shot didn't do much more than knock another of the things down, but the follow up shot blew a hole through its grinning skull.

The vicious little creatures scattered as I drove forward, blasting them with each working of the lever. I ran the Winchester dry, then drew my 1911 while I held the rifle with my off hand. I'd gotten pretty good at one-handed shooting, and I was glad that I'd loaded it with an iron mag. In a handful of shots, I was alone on the hillside again, the tiny corpses rapidly decomposing into dust where they'd fallen.

I paused, as the first spatters of rain landed on my shoulders, and reloaded.

The draw had fallen silent as the screeching of the monsters and the echoes of my gunshots had died away. The wind was still snatching at my shirt, but there was still an oppressive tension in the air.

Looking down, I thought over how to reload. The little goblin creatures had taken iron to kill, but I had no guarantees that they were all I was going to face. I put another iron mag in the pistol, then reloaded the rifle with my alternating loads again.

Then I headed down into the draw.

The shadows were deeper than last time. Whether that was because of the clouds, or because of what Riddle was doing down there, I didn't know. I had to step carefully and check every nook and cranny as I made my way toward the cave.

There was a dark haze around the cave mouth and, at first, I thought it was just shadows. As I got closer, though, I saw that those shadows were *writhing*.

Nothing leaped out at me, but as I studied what I was facing I realized it was something similar to the waves of sorcerous black smoke that Riddle had hit me with back in town. Needless to say, I didn't want to touch it, but I had to get in there.

Taking a deep breath, which stank of smoke, sulfur, and burned blood, I put a hand on the crucifix on my chest and bowed my head.

Lord, if You want me to stop this, I know that You will protect me.

Then, even though there'd been no sign to let me know it was going to be okay, knowing that I was the only one in a position to stop this, I surrendered in trust to the Most High and stepped toward the twisting shadows.

They receded, pulling back even more swiftly as I took my hand away from the crucifix, letting it hang in plain sight. I walked down into the cave, as the shadows closed in behind me, though they receded still more as I clamped my flashlight to my rifle's handguard and delved deeper.

Despite the gloom, I was moving faster than I had before. I avoided kicking any of the skulls as I passed them—there almost seemed to be more than I'd seen before, but there was no way the Killer could have moved *that* fast—

and moved with just enough caution that I was pretty sure I wasn't going to go headfirst into the pit when I got there.

I still almost did a gainer, stopping just short as the dark abyss yawned at my feet.

For a moment, I just stood there and cussed myself, because I'd gone back to town for rope and climbing stuff, and then had forgotten all about them in the rush to catch Riddle. I wasn't sure how I was going to get down there, assuming that Riddle had just floated down using his sorcerous levitation.

I'd missed something the last time I'd been down there, though. There was a spike driven into the rock at the back of the cave, a rope tied to it and falling away into the dark beneath. I could see a faint glow below, telling me that the pit went back a ways beneath my feet, and I could hear Riddle's voice, chanting syllables that put my teeth on edge.

I eyed the rope for a second, playing my light over it. It looked old, but it wasn't one of those nylon ropes, and I didn't see any fraying that would make me fear for my life taking it down. It wasn't all that far a drop if it *did* break, though I really didn't want to be off balance going down there, not with Riddle up to his tricks.

The Winchester 1886 hadn't been designed to be slung; there were no sling swivels, and I hadn't been inclined to mar the admittedly battered stock with new ones. My sling was a bit more ad hoc, mostly made of old, crusty paracord. It did the trick though, despite the fact that I rarely used it. Slinging the rifle across my back, taking a deep breath that quickly got shallow as the stench of sorcery bit the back of my nose, I started down.

The rope creaked under my weight, and I swayed as I worked my way down the rock face, slowly descending into the lurid red glow coming from the alcove where Riddle was conjuring whatever he was conjuring. The glow flickered weirdly, not like a fire, but almost as if something alive was swaying in time with his chanting.

That wasn't good.

That assessment was getting increasingly repetitive as this situation went on.

I reached the bottom, quickly pivoting away from the rock wall and drawing my .45. The Winchester might have hit a lot harder, but I was in close quarters, and it was faster to draw the handgun than try to unsling the rifle.

Something rolled beneath my boot, and I looked down, straining my eyes in the dim, shifting illumination. The floor of the cave was littered with bones.

Picking my steps carefully, I started forward. A passage led down, under where I'd approached the pit in the first place, curving off to my left. It was where the red glow was coming from.

The passage didn't turn out to be that long, though I estimated I'd gone down about fifty feet by the time I came around a corner and found myself at the entrance to a large chamber.

Still more skulls lined the walls, lit by a red, glowing figure in the center of the room. At first I thought it was Riddle, but he was crouched near the back. The apparition was tall and twisted, almost human in shape, but monstrously out of proportion. That was when it was visible as anything but a column of swaying flame. There was something deeply unsettling about it, and I wondered if I wasn't looking at Riddle's master. Something right out of the Abyss itself.

It didn't turn toward me or move to attack me, though I could *feel* that it was watching me. If it was the demon I thought it was, then it could regard me without need for eyes, anyway.

Riddle straightened as I stepped deeper into the chamber, my .45 trained on him. He didn't turn to look at me, but lifted his head, something in his hands in front of him.

Typical sorcerer. Drama kids, all of them.

"I have to admit, I can admire your persistence, Mr. Horn." The slightly hesitant tech guy was gone, replaced by a much more assured presence. "I had hoped that you might get up and follow me here, at least somewhat. You're a threat, certainly, but you are far too late. This will be awfully satisfying."

He turned and held up what was in his hands. "You still don't know what the Leutenburg Killer is, do you?"

The pieces fell into place as I saw what he was holding. It looked like a human heart, still fresh and beating, despite the fact that it wasn't connected to anything. I'd never encountered one of the Deathless, but I'd heard about them. That explained why the shapeshifter had gone to the gallows or the chair so many times and kept coming back.

Its life was bound to that heart, which it had ripped out and hidden in this cave. It would "die," resurrect around that heart, then get up, tear it out of its chest again, bury it in the box behind Riddle, and go back to murdering people for kicks. Who knew how old that thing really was?

He smiled as he watched me, still holding that grisly trophy. There was no real warmth or joy in that smile. It was the expression of a shark, an inhuman predator. Riddle had left his soul behind a long time ago. He'd been able to mask it for a while, but now he saw no reason to pretend anymore.

"You understand, now." The smile widened, which only served to make him look more demented. "Can you imagine it?" He was getting excited. "What I could do with one of the Deathless at my beck and call?" He held up the heart, studying it in the light cast by the spirit in the center of the room. "I hold its very life in my hands. You made it easier, you know, putting it down the way you did. I should thank you." He tittered. "It doesn't mean I won't feed you to it, once it resurrects again."

I could feel the fiery being in the center of the room turning its attention to me, but then it seemed to flinch aside, almost as if its invisible eyes had lit on the crucifix around my neck and recoiled. Riddle didn't seem to notice, and I hid a grim smile. This wasn't going to go the way he thought.

With a silent prayer to the Most High, all the angels, and all the saints, I lifted my 1911 just as Riddle raised the heart even higher, admiring it and thinking about the vile things he was going to do with it.

The bullet knocked the heart out of his hand, flinging it into the back of the cave.

I had iron-tipped rounds in the .45, of course, thanks to the confrontation with the malignant gnomes outside, so the shot didn't do much real damage to the heart. The shock as the bullet ripped the thing out of Riddle's hand, however, threw the entire room into confusion.

He screamed, ducking away and snatching his hand into his armpit as if he'd been burned. The thing in the middle of the room suddenly flared up, growing wider as if it was going to engulf the entire chamber, but I held up the crucifix and shouted a Gloria Patri, at which it recoiled, screamed with a strange crackling noise, and disappeared into the floor, leaving my flashlight as the only source of illumination.

I charged Riddle, intent on getting him down and neutralized before he could pull any new occult tricks out of his voluminous sleeves. He had twisted and fallen to his knees, tripping over his robes as he tried to get to a small bag lying next to the ancient chest he'd apparently taken the heart out of. I hit him halfway there, driving my knee into his ribs and slamming him against the chest, knocking the antique over and cracking the lid.

He squawked as he hit and a hand came out of his robes with a knife. It wasn't much of a knife, more like a prison shank, but I knew that I didn't want to get cut with that thing. There was no telling what Riddle had done with it, what kind of evil was attached to it, but I could guess.

I stepped back rapidly as he lunged toward me, slashing with the knife.

There is a school of thought that, especially when dealing with the mortal instruments of the demons of the Abyss, that we should take every step possible to stop them without killing them. More than just their lives and the lives and sanity of the people nearby are at stake. Their souls are at stake.

However, most of those people opining about that have never had anyone trying to stab them, let alone with a cursed knife.

I shot him through the teeth at about three feet, just as the knife swished through the air inches from my stomach. Against a human being, the iron or silver bearing in the hollow point didn't matter a bit. His head snapped back, the spray of blood and shattered bone almost invisible in the low light from my flashlight, and he fell on his face, the knife falling from his hands.

It was tempting to relax at that point, as the strange shadows seemed to dive into the ground after the flaming apparition, and I blinked in the suddenly redoubled cone of light splashing against the corpse, the scattered bones, and the upended chest.

Then the chest stirred, and I heard something move, a rasping, scratching sound.

I had no idea how long it took one of the Deathless to resurrect. From the sounds of things, though, and the looks of things, as a clawlike hand reached out of the chest and scratched at the ground, a low, hissing moan going through the cave, it didn't take long at all.

Unslinging my Winchester, I tried to remember whether it was an iron or a silver round in the chamber, as I stepped toward the back of the thing's lair, pivoting to keep my eyes on the chest and the monster unfolding itself from it while I tried not to trip or fall over the bones scattered on the rocky floor.

The Deathless—whatever its name had once been, long ago—still resembled a man, if horribly emaciated and hairless. It twisted its head almost one hundred eighty degrees around to glare at me, its eyes completely black, a lipless mouth filled with shark teeth.

I spared it just enough of a look to make sure I had some distance, and that it hadn't suddenly gotten quick enough to close the distance while I blinked. It still seemed to be disoriented and slow, though, barely able to move. It was almost like watching a Claymation puppet.

There was no way that was going to last, though. I tore my eyes away from it as it continued dragging itself out of the tipped-over chest, casting eyes and light onto the floor at the back of the cave.

I couldn't see what I was looking for at first. The bones were stacked even deeper back there, and I'd kind of lost track of directions and distances during the short but frenetic fight with Riddle.

Bones scattered with a rattle as the Deathless finished crawling out, its movements getting faster and smoother, though it seemed it still couldn't stand. I started kicking bones aside, desperate in the heat of the moment. I'd pray for the dead later.

There. I put the muzzle of the Winchester against the dirt-encrusted heart and pulled the trigger.

The report of the .45-70 was deafening in that stone-walled space, but it was nothing compared to the scream that was ripped from the monster that had just reached its feet, as the heart spattered into red mush under the impact of the heavy chunk of lead.

Pivoting back toward the monster, I pinned it with rifle muzzle and light. I almost needn't have bothered.

Already collapsed onto its knees, the Deathless—deathless no more—clutched its sunken chest as it started to wither. The scream was already fading into a wheeze, as centuries of decay took over in seconds. Flesh melted against the bones, shrinking and drying before crumbling away, and finally, only a skeleton with a weirdly deformed skull lay on the floor next to the chest.

Looking around the cave, which was now only a hole in the ground full of human bones, I sighed, made the sign of the cross, and started toward the exit.

Yep. Father Gascone was going to have a *lot* of work to do when he rolled back into town for the weekend Masses.

Author's Note

Thank you for reading *Something in the Dark*. It's been a while since I've stepped into Jed's shoes, but the absence hasn't made the Otherworld any less dark and creepy. I hope you enjoyed it.

To keep up-to-date, I hope that you'll sign up for my newsletter—[you get a free American Praetorians novella, *Drawing the Line*, when you do.](#)

If you've enjoyed this novel, I hope that you'll go leave a review on Amazon or Goodreads. Reviews matter a lot to independent authors, so I appreciate the effort.

If you'd like to connect, I have a Facebook page at https://www.facebook.com/PeteNealenAuthor. I'm also on Twitter at https://twitter.com/AmericanPraeto2. You can also contact me, or just read my musings and occasional samples on the blog, at https://www.americanpraetorians.com. I look forward to hearing from you.

Also By Peter Nealen

The Jed Horn Supernatural Thriller Series
Nightmares
A Silver Cross and a Winchester
The Walker on the Hills
The Canyon of the Lost (Novelette)
Older and Fouler Things

The Lost Series
Ice and Monsters
Shadows and Crows
Darkness and Stone
Swords Against the Night
The Alchemy of Treason
The Rock of Battle

The Edge of Imperium Series
Spheres of Influence
Cascade Effect
Brink of Destruction (forthcoming)

Brave New Disorder (Pallas Group Solutions Thrillers)
Gray War
The Dragon and the Skull
Silver or Lead
Frontiers of Chaos
Non-State Actor

Galaxy's Edge – Order of the Centurion
Always Legion

The Brannigan's Blackhearts Universe
Kill Yuan
The Colonel Has A Plan (Online Short)
Fury in the Gulf

Burmese Crossfire
Enemy Unidentified
Frozen Conflict
High Desert Vengeance
Doctors of Death
Kill or Capture
Enemy of My Enemy
War to the Knife
Blood Debt
Marque and Reprisal
Concrete Jungle
Legacy of Terror

The Maelstrom Rising Series

Escalation
Holding Action
Crimson Star
Strategic Assets
Fortress Doctrine
Thunder Run
Area Denial
Power Vacuum
Option Zulu
SPOTREPS – A Maelstrom Rising Anthology

The Unity Wars Series

The Fall of Valdek
The Defense of Provenia
The Alliance Rises

The American Praetorians Series

Drawing the Line: An American Praetorians Story (Novella)
Task Force Desperate
Hunting in the Shadows
Alone and Unafraid

The Devil You Don't Know
Lex Talionis

www.ingramcontent.com/pod-product-compliance
Lightning Source LLC
LaVergne TN
LVHW041808060526
838201LV00046B/1168